Joseph P. Smith

McKinley - the People's Choice

The congratulations of the country, the calls of delegations at Canton, the

addresses by them. His eloquent and effective responses. - Vol. 1

Joseph P. Smith

McKinley - the People's Choice
The congratulations of the country, the calls of delegations at Canton, the
addresses by them. His eloquent and effective responses. - Vol. 1

ISBN/EAN: 9783337234461

Printed in Europe, USA, Canada, Australia, Japan

Cover: Foto ©Andreas Hilbeck / pixelio.de

More available books at **www.hansebooks.com**

THE CONGRATULATIONS OF THE COUNTRY,

THE CALLS OF DELEGATIONS AT CANTON,

THE ADDRESSES BY THEM.

HIS ELOQUENT AND EFFECTIVE RESPONSES.

FULL TEXT OF EACH SPEECH OR ADDRESS MADE BY HIM

FROM JUNE 18 TO AUGUST 1, 1896.

COMPILED FOR THE REPUBLICAN NATIONAL COMMITTEE
By JOSEPH P. SMITH.

The Repository Press, Canton, O.
1896.

McKINLEY AS A CANDIDATE.

THE JOLLIFICATION AT CANTON.

THE nomination of WILLIAM McKINLEY as the Republican candidate for President has been ratified more generally and enthusiastically by all classes of his fellow citizens, the country over, than perhaps that of any other candidate of his or any party in our history. On the afternoon and evening of Thursday, June 18th, the day on which he was nominated, Canton, Ohio, his home, was alive with delighted people. It had been arranged that the citizens of Canton should assemble in the Public Square, immediately on receipt of the news from St. Louis, form a brigade, and march to the McKinley residence, on North Market Street. But the people took the matter into their own hands; regardless of plans or programmes in the exuberance of their joy they rushed *en masse* and pell mell to the Major's home, from every direction and street and square in the city. The decisive ballot at St. Louis was not yet finished before they had assembled by thousands, blocked North Market Street, crowded upon the lawn and surrounded his residence, and were surging through it, with every possible manifestation of satisfaction and delight. Even before the arrival of the brigade from the Square, not a quarter of a mile distant, Major McKINLEY was obliged to come out and acknowledge the deafening calls of his neighbors and friends. When the column from down town had forced its way up the crowded street, he was again compelled to appear, and Hon. F. E. CASE, a prominent manufacturer, made the following address:

"Major McKINLEY: Your neighbors and townsmen wish to be the first to congratulate you upon your nomination to the highest office within the gift of the people of the United States. None know better than these neighbors here assembled how well this honor is merited. They were the first to witness the beginning of your public career. They saw you quit your academic studies, with the ardor of youth, and a bravery beyond your years, to devote your services to your imperilled country. The courage and ability you then displayed, a promise of what followed in later years, won for you that rank and title by which we have so long and familiarly addressed you. A few of your veteran comrades have again formed in line, and, joining the citizens of Canton, take this opportunity to make pronounced their high regard for you. The ability and fidelity with which you have discharged great public trusts, and the recognition by your countrymen of long and useful service to the State and Nation, are exceedingly gratifying to your Canton and Stark County friends. We welcome you as neighbors, without distinction of party, bearing in mind, that, while you have acted in a broader field, you have not lost sight of the duties and obligations of the citizen, and that with your many cares and responsibilities you have always found time and opportunity to lend your valued assistance to all that makes for good in our community. We unite in extending to you our hearty congratulations and good wishes."

Major McKinley's Response.

Mounting a chair on his doorstep, Major McKinley faced the thousands of his expectant and joyous fellow citizens, and when the storm of applause had sufficiently subsided to make himself heard, he spoke as follows:

"My Friends and Fellow Citizens: I am greatly honored by this demonstration. Its non-partisan character forbids political discussion, and I appear only to make grateful acknowledgment for your address and congratulations. I am not indifferent to the pleasure which you exhibit at the news just received from the Republican National Convention. For days your interest has been centered upon St. Louis, and your presence in such vast numbers here this afternoon testifies your personal good will to myself and family, as well as your gratification with the work there done. Your cordial assurances are the more highly appreciated by me because they come from my fellow citizens—men of every party, my old army comrades, my neighbors and former constituents—with whom I have lived almost a life time, and who have honored me over and over again with important public trusts. Your warm words of greeting are heartily reciprocated and will be cherished forever. Many of those around me have not always agreed with me touching political questions; but it is pleasant, as I look into your faces, to recall that in all the years of the past there has never been a moment when you have withheld from me your friendship, encouragement and confidence. You have always been as generous as loyal, and my heart is full of gratitude to all of you.

"There is nothing, it seems to me, more gratifying, or more honorable, to any man, than to have the regard of his fellow townsmen, and in this I feel that I am and have always been peculiarly blessed. Never were neighbors more devoted or unfaltering in their support to any one than you have been to me. You have made my cause your cause, and my home among you has been in consequence one of constant and ever increasing pleasure. This county and city are very near and dear to me; here I have spent my life since early manhood, so that I have been identified with this magnificent county for now nearly a third of a century. I have followed its growth with the fondest pride and noted with peculiar satisfaction that it has kept pace with the most advanced and prosperous communities. I am especially glad to greet you here at the house where our married life began, and our children were born—and in this feeling I know Mrs. McKinley heartily joins; our greatest joys and deepest sorrows are ineffaceably connected with this home and city. You have never failed to greet me with your best wishes and congratulations upon every occasion of my nomination or election to a public office, commencing twenty years ago, when I was first named by my party for Congress. I can not undertake to estimate the value of these many friendly demonstrations, so encouraging, so helpful, so inspiring—far beyond what you could have anticipated or believed at the time. Your call to-day, though not entirely unexpected, is most highly appreciated, and I thank you from the heart for what you have said, as expressive of the feelings of yourself, sir, and those for whom you speak. This latest evidence of your esteem makes me more indebted to you than ever and the happy memory of your kindness and confidence will abide with me forever."

ALLIANCE SECOND TO GREET HIM.

In forty-five minutes from the time Major McKinley's nomination was assured by the deciding vote of the Ohio delegation in the St. Louis Convention, two thousand citizens of Alliance and Eastern Stark County, coming twenty miles by special train on the Pittsburg, Fort Wayne and Chicago Railroad, stood at his door in Canton, and offered their heartiest congratulations, through Hon. S. J. Williams, State Senator from this district. The run had been made from Alliance in twenty minutes and ten full companies of citizens and students from Mt. Union College were in line. Major McKinley spoke briefly in reply to the address of Mr. Williams, thanking the people for their personal good will, but making no reference to politics.

MASSILLON AND AKRON.

The crowd had begun to disperse, but its attention was re-arrested by the arrival of a monster delegation from Massillon and Western Stark County, which came by special train on the Interurban Electric Railway. Nineteen cars were jammed with people, hundreds of whom were employes of Russell & Co's great machine shops. Dozens could not get into the cars but clung to the sides and tops of the coaches, despite danger and inconvenience. They reached Canton at 7:15 and marched at once to Major McKinley's residence, where Mr. E. A. Jones, of Cleveland, formerly Superintendent of the Massillon Public Schools, made a speech of congratulation, "both on what he had done, and what was deservedly in store for him, as the faithful friend and servant of the people " To this Major McKinley responded that he was "deeply grateful for their words of encouragement and cheer, and that he was always glad to hear from and meet the laboring men of Massillon, and all his friends in that city. I remember well," said he, "that when I was given my first public trust (his nomination for Prosecuting Attorney twenty-seven years ago, the suggestion first came from Western Stark County, and 1 am proud of the fact that since then you have given me your loyal and unswerving support through the whole of my public career. I bid you all welcome, and good night."

By this time the Akron delegation was beginning to arrive. It reached Canton at 7:40, via the Cleveland, Terminal and Valley Railroad, in four special trains of ten coaches each. Fully four thousand men were in line, and the scenes as they marched through the streets to the music of bands, and on their arrival at the McKinley residence, were those of indescribable enthusiasm. Capt. Paul E. Werner, a prominent German publisher of Akron and Chief Marshal of the evening, spoke for the visitors from Summit County. He said:

"Major McKinley: These men come from the city of Akron. Among them are hundreds of personal friends whom you have known for many years. We consider you as one of our number. When your nomination was announced in our city it required but an hour's notice for them to congregate at the railroad station; they left their workshops, their homes, their stores, their offices, to hasten to congratulate you 1 introduce, fellow-townsmen, Major William McKinley, the nominee of the Republican National Convention, and our next President of the United States." (Wild cheering and applause.)

5

Major McKinley's Response.

The demonstration continued for several minutes, but when quiet was somewhat restored, Major McKinley spoke as follows:

"Capt. Werner and My Fellow Citizens: The crowd is so great that I fear I will not be able to make myself heard. I only appear that I may thank you for your gracious words and sentiments, as representing the citizens of Akron and Summit County. We are not strangers, but neighbors for many, many years past. More than once Summit County was part of the Congressional district I had the honor to represent. I remember twelve years ago, that I opened the campaign in Copley; I recollect, too, that in 1893, I opened the campaign in the State of Ohio, as the Republican candidate for Governor, in the city of Akron, and I cannot but believe that it is a good omen to have Akron and Summit County with us in any cause. I welcome you here to-night, and beg to express my warm appreciation of your coming thus early to tender me your congratulations. In this great audience are some of my old constituents of the 18th Ohio District—the first district that I had the honor to represent in Congress. Little Carroll, too, which I see is represented here, never failed to roll up a splendid majority for me, no matter what other counties might do for the Republican party and its cause. Indeed, this seems to be a spotaneous reunion of my old Congressional district, and I bid you hearty welcome to my home. You have long had my heart, and I thank you, and bid you good night."

CARROLLTON, OSNABURG, MINERVA AND NILES

Meanwhile five coaches of passengers had arrived from Carrollton, Osnaburg, Minerva, and vicinity, after forty miles ride on a special train via the Cleveland, Canton and Southern Railroad. It had left Carrollton, the county seat of Carroll County, at 6:40 Thursday evening, and reached Canton two hours later. About six hundred men were in line under command of Capt. W. F. Butler, recently sheriff of Carroll County. They marched at once to the McKinley residence, where they were greeted pleasantly by Major and Mrs. McKinley, whence they soon joined the rejoicing thousands who were marching about the city in groups and companies, singing and shouting as they went. The booming of artillery, the clanging of bells, and the shrieking of whistles had gradually given way to the more melodious but no less boisterous shouts and songs of the multitude.

A hundred citizens of Niles, Trumbull County, Ohio, the birthplace of Major McKinley, sixty miles away, arrived by special train at ten o'clock, Thursday night, and called to tender him their fervent congratulations. The Major thanked the visitors and shook hands with all of them, as he had so many thousands of others during the course of the afternoon and evening. He was late in retiring, but hundreds of the happy throng continued to jollify all night long. It is safe to say that he spoke to or greeted personally more than 50,000 people, between five o'clock and midnight. Never had Canton known so great a day in all her history.

CANTON REPUBLICANS AT HOME AGAIN.

The announcement of the expected return of Canton's contingent at St. Louis, Friday afternoon, July 19th, was the signal for a renewal of the demonstrations which had commenced Thursday evening and continued throughout the night. The newly organized escort of the First Ward Republican Club was first on the street, and the horsemen made a splendid appearance heading the parades. With this addition the evening was almost a duplicate of Thursday night. "Here they come; there is Canton!"—and the cheers which had been held in reserve for the Canton people all afternoon broke forth in mighty volume as the long column appeared in view. In a short time swarms of men and women filled every available inch of ground in the McKinley yard. Following closely upon the Canton people were delegations from Youngstown and Warren, in which were about five hundred people, and these commingled with the immense throng. It had been arranged that Major McKinley should address these delegations from the front veranda, but he went to the north side of his house to better accommodate the combined delegations. The Warren contingent, with many from Niles and Poland, were headed by the Warren band. The visiting delegations represented the industrial interests of the Mahoning Valley, and visited Canton for the sole purpose of congratulating Major McKinley and assuring him that their untiring labors were pledged to a victorious result at the polls next November. There was a large representation of the Giddings Republican Club of Warren, and of the Republican Central Committee of Trumbull County.

Major McKinley's appearance with Hon. William R. Day, Judge George E. Baldwin, and Congressman Robert W. Tayler was the signal for an outburst of cheers from thousands of throats that rivaled those of the previous evening. After quiet had been obtained, Mr. C. A. Yates, of Massillon, mounted the improvised platform and in a short address, presented Hon. Robert W. Tayler, of Lisbon, Columbiana County, Major McKinley's successor in the lower house of Congress, who said: "While we have not the good fortune to be first to congratulate you on the honor the Republican party has bestowed upon you, we rejoice to know we are the vanguard of the returning host that witnessed the splendid demonstration whereby you were nominated for President. The recollection of that scene will never be effaced from our minds There we saw the Republican party place you in nomination, and while it honored you it honored itself, and gave permanency to the wish that has been in the hearts of the American people for many months. This delegation left Canton with rising hopes that have been amply fulfilled. You are not only loved at home, but wherever the American flag floats. Twenty years ago Stark County gave you to Congress, four years ago she gave you to the State, and now she gives you to the Nation which has been your constant care. We know that the constancy, honor and patriotism which have distinguished you to this hour will characterize you ever more. You are first in the hearts of your countrymen, not because you are a Presidential nominee, but because as that nominee you so conspicuously represent the great principle whose triumph is their chief concern as well as yours. That you may receive every blessing that a life well spent can bring, is the wish of those about me.

7

Following Congressmen TAYLER, Mr. YATES presented Judge GEORGE E. BALDWIN, who spoke in behalf of Stark County. He said:

"Major McKINLEY: Language fails me as I attempt to convey to you the congratulations of those of your neighbors and friends who for over twenty years have watched with interest your wonderful progress. On last Saturday about three hundred of your neighbors and friends concluded they would go to St. Louis, and they took with them their bag and baggage, determined to remain there until you were nominated; and of the wonderful influence they had in bringing about this great result modesty forbids me to speak. (Laughter and applause.) If you could have seen the great throngs of people that assembled at the Union Depot in St. Louis on Sunday afternoon and have heard their expressions, and could have seen the McKinley badges upon the coats of four-fifths of the great crowd that gathered you would then have had an idea of the intense interest the masses of the people have in you and in the welfare of this country. On the day that the Convention assembled, if you could have seen the thousands upon thousands of intelligent faces looking toward the Great Convention that was to meet that day, anxious and eager that some measure should be adopted and the man nominated that they believed was most certain to bring back prosperity to them, you would have been inspired by the interest and great efforts of your party to bring about those grand results, which, I am pleased to say, were fully accomplished. I remember when you first came into public life; many of us here were present when you were nominated for Prosecuting Attorney, and well, faithfully, boldly and honestly did you discharge your duties. By more than twenty years of faithful, honest and able service you have endeared yourself to all good people, not only of this vicinity, but the country at large. During the time of your service in Congress prosperity perched upon the banners of our people; the wheels of industry revolved, and the whistles of the workshop told of the happy condition of the American laborer, whose toil was everywhere sought and always remunerated by a good day's wages. But the Democratic party was allowed to come into power. Then the scene changed—the wheels of industry ceased to revolve, the hum of the spindle died out, the whistle of the factory was soon silenced. The people began to ask that party to fulfill its promises; they called aloud for work—even for bread, but the echo was the only answer to their wailing cry. Then they looked again to the Republican party and to the man who had always championed and so bravely battled for protection, to bring back those industries and that prosperity. They turned their faces to you, sir, the great people of this Nation arose in their might and demanded you for their standard bearer. (Tremendous cheering.) The Convention at St. Louis listened to their cry; they felt that this is the year of the people—the people had spoken and the great party of the people was bound to obey their behests. They yesterday placed you in nomination as the leader of the greatest party of the greatest nation upon the face of the earth. Already we have some evidences of returning prosperity; (cheers) the rising sun of prosperity has already thrown upon the lattice window of hope his early smile and the wage earners begin to rejoice at the prospect. As soon as this can be fully realized, they will flock to your support, and when the old party is in power again, it will come to stay. (Loud cheers) They have selected you as their standard bearer, and regardless of party, faith or creed, they will rally and elect you as President of the United States. (Vociferous cheering.) No man has ever stood as near the hearts of the people, since the days of the matchless and immortal LINCOLN, as you. We confide the care, the custody and the keeping of the industries of the people of this country and their prosperity to you. We believe you will be elected, by the greatest majority any President ever received, (continued cheering), and that you will faithfully, honestly and ably conduct the affairs of this great and glorious Nation until prosperity shall perch on its banners ev'r more." (Loud and continuous applause.)

The appearance of Judge WILLIAM R. DAY, of Canton, as he stepped upon the platform, was the signal for another burst of cheers. His remarks were most appropriate, eloquent and tender, and greatly affected all his hearers, especially his esteemed friend, Major McKINLEY, who was moved to tears by them. He said:

"Major McKINLEY: I speak to you, not as the Governor of Ohio, or the President of the United States—that surely, you shall be,—but I claim the great privilege on behalf of these, your old friends, of still addressing you as 'neighbor.' For we have not forgotten that in all these years of success, and while your fame has spread to the uttermost corners of the civilized world, and you now 'stand on fortune's crowning slope,' to us you have always been the companion, the counselor, the guide, and familiar friend. Greater tribute than this can no man bring. Those who know you best, love you most. To-day we had a very pleasant surprise in a gift of these flowers from some ladies of Richmond to your most gracious and noble wife. (Cheers.) I am proud, sir, that this representative lady, when she brought them in, said 'Governor McKINLEY is in the heart of every good mother and every good wife in all this broad land (continued applause), and we send these flowers to his noble wife as some slight expression of our appreciation of him and good will to her. These flowers are typical of the purity of his life and character, as unsullied as his honor, and as fragrant as his good name ' Major McKINLEY accept these flowers for Mrs. McKINLEY, from the ladies of Richmond, Ind , with their best wishes for her health and prosperity, and your continued success." (Applause.)

Major McKinley's Response.

Major McKINLEY was escorted to the stand amid deafening cheers, and gave evidence of great emotion when he spoke, as follows:

"MY FELLOW CITIZENS: How can I make fitting response to the splendid tributes which have been paid me by my earliest friends? I think I might be excused by merely saying that I am inadequate to the task, and can only express my gratitude by the silence due to a full and overflowing heart. I have experienced many touching incidents in my life. Yesterday immediately after the nomination I was surrounded by my neighbors and fellow citizens of Canton, who did not go to St. Louis, and by friends from Alliance and Massillon, and then came 4 000 more from Akron last night. With all these tokens, I was deeply and profoundly impressed, but somehow the words spoken by these gentlemen, and surrounded as I am by their associates who journeyed with them to St. Louis—somehow they have touched me more deeply, sounded the depths of my heart more surely, than anything that has gone before. In this audience I see representatives from all of the counties which constitute the Congressional district with which I have been associated all my life. A large number of my fellow citizens are here from Trumbull County, the place of my birth. (Great applause.) A large number are here from Mahoning County (cheers from Mahoning citizens), the place where I spent my boyhood, the

9

county where I received my education, and from which I enlisted in the war for the preservation of the Union, away back in 1861. (Loud and continuous cheering.) And then around me are the later friends, for from Mahoning County I came to Stark, nearly thirty years ago. You have all been my friends ever since; I am proud to include among my immediate friends not only the good people of Stark, Mahoning and Trumbull, but all the grand old Western Reserve, which was so long represented in the National Congress by GIDDINGS and WADE, and the gifted and immortal GARFIELD. (Applause.) And now, my friends and fellow citizens, I know that you will excuse me—I want only to add, in terms of sincere affection, that I thank each and every one of you from my heart for these manifestations of your friendship, devotion and loyalty and as you seem to have brought back what you went for, those whom you left behind want me to say that they are glad to see you home again."

GREETINGS FROM THE EMPIRE STATE.

The McKinley League of the State of New York arrived from St. Louis via the Pennsylvania lines, at Coshocton, Ohio, on Friday, June 19th, and came to Canton that evening on a special train over the C., C. and S. R. R. They chose Hon. JOHN E. MILHOLLAND, of the New York Tribune, as spokesman and marched at once to the McKinley residence, where Mr. MILHOLLAND climbed on a chair and presented to Major McKINLEY the friends before him. Hon. WARNER MILLER, of Herkimer, was first introduced, and spoke as follows:

"LADIES AND GENTLEMEN: We thought it proper on our way home from the St. Louis Convention to call here and pay our respects to the man who had been honored by the Republican party, he who is your fellow townsman and neighbor. It has been my privilege to know Major McKINLEY for nearly twenty years and it affords me great pleasure to assure him on behalf of the Republicans of New York that we shall give to him and to the principles he represents, the largest majority in November that has ever been given to any Presidential candidate since the organization of the Government. (Loud cheers.) The Republicans of New York will be second to none in the whole country in their loyalty to the party, and in their efforts and labors for its success. We have but a moment to spend here and therefore I do not wish to take up your time in making a speech. I came here simply to take the hand of Major McKINLEY and to assure him of the affection and love of the people of New York. And now, gentleman of the McKinley League of the Empire State, it gives me great pleasure to introduce to you Major WILLIAM McKINLEY, the next President of the United States." (Applause.)

Major McKinley's Response.

When comparative silence had been restored, Major McKINLEY said:

"MY FELLOW CITIZENS OF NEW YORK: It gives me very great pleasure to meet and greet you here at my home today. It was most gracious on your part to pause in your journey to the East long enough to give me the pleasure of meeting you face to face; and nothing could have been more agreeable to me than to be presented to the members of the McKinley League of the State of New York, by my old friend, long a member of the House of Rep-·

resentatives, and Senator at Washington—Hon. WARNER MILLER. (Long applause.) I am always glad to meet and greet him. All we have to do this year, my fellow citizens, is to keep close to the people. (Loud cheering.) To hearken to the voice of the people and have faith in the people, and if we do that the people will win for us a triumph for the great principles which in all the years of the past have given us plenty and prosperity." (Great cheering.)

When the Major stopped speaking, Mr. MILHOLLAND again mounted a chair and introduced Hon. GEORGE E. MATTHEWS, of Buffalo, President of the New York McKinley League. Mr. MATTHEWS' voice was exceedingly hoarse; he explained the circumstance by saying that it had become so by shouting for McKINLEY, and assured the Major that his voice would be restored in time to make speeches in his behalf and shout again when the victory was won next November. At the conclusion of the speeches, Mr. MILHOLLAND exhibited the famous "Ferris Wheel Petition," which consisted of five and three-fourth miles of paper, and contained the signatures of 247,000 people of the State of New York asking for the nomination of WILLIAM McKINLEY for President. Mrs. McKINLEY and Mother McKINLEY joined the Major and an impromptu reception was held at the front door of the residence, during which many of the New Yorkers were received by the family. A pleasing incident of this reception was the presentation of a handsome badge to Mrs. McKINLEY, on behalf of the women of New York, who extended their heartfelt congratulations. Mrs. McKINLEY received the souvenir with a smile and graceful bow, expressive alike of her own pleasure and the thanks of herself and family.

A DELEGATION OF COLORED CALLERS

In company with the New York Republican League, which called upon Major McKINLEY, June 19th, was a delegation representing the Colored Republican League of New York State. They were cordially received by him, and a congratulatory address in writing was presented by Rev Dr. ERNEST LYON, Pastor of St. Mark's Methodist Episcopal Church, of New York City, and President of the Preachers' Alliance. In behalf of the colored Republicans, Dr. LYON said:

"To the Hon. WILLIAM McKINLEY: We are here as a body of colored American citizens, representing various organizations in the Empire State. We have come with our fellow citizens to congratulate you on your nomination as the standard bearer of the grand old Republican party, and to assure you that we shall return to our respective homes to labor zealously for the success of the ticket nominated by the representatives of the people in convention assembled at St. Louis."

Signed on behalf of the Ministerial Alliance, ERNEST LYON, (D. D.) President; ALFRED C. COWAN, President Colored Republican Association of New York; EDWARD E. LEE, Assistant Sergeant-at-Arms at the Republican Convention, St. Louis, J. H. SIMMS, Editor and Publisher of the New York Central Echo, and President of the Henry Highland Garrett Republican Club, New York City; A. M. THOMAS, attorney-at-law, Buffalo, N. Y.; SAMUEL MORGAN, President Colored Republican County Club of New York City; ALFRED J. SCOTT, of the Eleventh Assembly District, and J. A. SMITH, of the Twenty-fifth Assembly District

11

MORE NEW YORK MEN.

The visit to Major McKinley of the New York State McKinley League on Friday evening, was followed Saturday morning, June 20th, by that of another distinguished party from the metropolis, *en route* home from St. Louis, at 8:12 o'clock, via the Ft. Wayne railroad. The party was composed of the following gentlemen: Hon. Cornelius N. Bliss, President American Protective Tariff League; General Horace Porter, President Union League, New York City; General Anson G. McCook, Chamberlain, New York City; General Charles H. T. Collis, Commissioner of Public Works; Colonel S. V. R. Cruger, President of the Park Commission; Frank D. Pavey, ex-State Senator; Richard J. Lewis, and Robert Miller, ex-members of the New York Assembly; Hon. William Brookfield and Andrew Jacobs, members New York State Committee; and Messrs. Henry C. Robinson, William S. Bragg, Thomas F. Eagan, Benjamin Oppenheimer, William Henckel, John G. Graham, Andrew P. Dedi, Thomas Humphrey, J. E. McMillen, Montague Leslie, J. F. McGowan and Lloyd Collis. Hon. James R. Garfield, of Mentor, the Republican leader of the Ohio State Senate, also accompanied the party. They were cordially received by Major and Mrs. McKinley, and a number of the party called on Mother McKinley at her home on West Tuscarawas street, before the departure of their train at 1:21 that afternoon.

GREETINGS FROM THE TIN WORKERS OF NILES.

Saturday, June 20th, was a day of tin buckets, banners, canes, whistles and horns—and speeches. The operatives of the tin plate industries of Niles, Ohio, paid their respects to the statesman whom they pronounce their greatest friend and champion. The visitors were decorated with the badges of the Niles McKinley League and tin souvenirs; they carried tin canes, with medalions of McKinley as heads. The party was composed chiefly of the operatives of the Falcon Tin Plate Factory, which has been in operation ever since the enactment of the McKinley Law gave proper protection to this industry. They bore two large streamers, or sheets of tin, like banners, nearly as long as the line of paraders, on one of which was the inscription, "From Niles to the White House," and on the other, "Who Made the Niles Tin Mill? The McKinley Bill, Of Course." All along the line of march the cheering by both paraders and spectators was most vociferous. The Niles men have a yell which is peculiar to themselves. It is, 'Rah, Rah, Right." "Who's all right?" "McKinley's all right." "Where was he born? N-I-L-E-S"! This was repeated frequently. Apt, as it may seem, Niles, the birthplace of Major McKinley, is the location of large tin plate industries. Mr. Joseph Smith, chairman of the meeting, presented Col. William H. Smiley, as Major McKinley appeared on the veranda of his residence, who said:

"Major McKinley: I have the pleasure of introducing to you some hundreds of the citizens of your native town of Niles. Among them is a very large number of the employes of our town. We realize that what we have been, what we are, and what we hope to be, is largely due to that which is now called Protection, but that sometimes has been called 'McKinleyism.' (Cheers.) We realize not only what you have done for us, but what it has cost you to do it. We know what it must have cost a

12

man in the Fifty-first Congress, which gave us our tin mill. (Loud and vociferous cheering.) We know that you would have sacrificed every interest and given your life to your country, and to us, and if there is anything we can do for you we want to do it. In 1891 the candidate for Governor who opposed you, stood on the platform of a car in our town and said to the citizens of Niles: 'No man will ever live to see tin made in Niles,' (at this moment a tremendous rattling of the tin banners carried by the Niles delegation was heard) but that is only one of the many mistakes our adversaries have made. Every Republican President, and every man who has led the Republican party to victory since the days of LINCOLN, was (perhaps, strangely enough,) born in Ohio. Major McKINLEY will be the fifth and when there will add to the glory of being born in Ohio—and especially of having been born in Niles. (Loud cheering.) What can the Nation do except to do as that Convention did, and elect him unanimously? Gentlemen, I now introduce you to Major McKINLEY." (Three rousing cheers were given him.)

Major McKinley's Response.

The Major stepped upon a chair and bowed his acknowledgements for the great applause that greeted him. He recognized among the hundreds of the citizens of his birthplace, and the thousands of others crowding into the yard, the face of an old friend of his boyhood days, and did not forget it. He said:

"Mr. SMILEY, AND MY FELLOW CITIZENS: I am very glad indeed to meet so many citizens of my native town. I do not find many of the faces that I used to know in my boyhood in this audience, but I think I have been able to see one that I remember to have seen in the village of Niles when I was a boy, and that is HENRY MASON'S. I recollect him as the merchant of the town, and as I look into his face to-day, I remember that he was kind to every boy—and I like a man who is kind to boys—(loud cheering)—and am especially pleased to meet him here again, after a lapse of forty years, in my home at Canton. I am glad to meet and greet so many of the workingmen of the thriving little city of Niles. I am glad to have demonstrated in my native town that we can make tin plate in the United States, and in reply to what your spokesman has been kind enough to say of my efforts in that connection, I answer that if I have been associated with any legislation that has given to a single American working-man a day's work at American wages which he did not receive before, that is honor enough for me. (Loud and continuous applause.) What we want in this country is a policy that will give to every American workingman full work at American wages. A policy that will put enough money into the Treasury of the United States to run the Government. A policy that will bring back to us such a period of prosperity and of plenty as that we enjoyed for more than thirty years prior to 1893. I am glad to welcome you all to my home; it is especially pleasant to have the men from my boyhood town and the place of my birth gather around me as they have to-day, and I reciprocate most warmly all the kind sentiments that have been so generously spoken in your behalf by your Chairman. I wish for old Niles prosperity in every workshop and factory, and in every home, love, contentment and happiness. I thank you, and bid you good afternoon." (Three prolonged cheers for Major McKINLEY were again given.)

WORKINGMEN FROM WHEELING, WEST VIRGINIA.

A delegation of workingmen from Wheeling, West Virginia, took up the celebration, Saturday afternoon, June 20th, where the Niles tin workers left off, and right royally did they salute Major McKinley. Fully fifteen hundred enthusiastic, shouting Wheeling workingmen appeared at Major McKinley's home shortly after five o'clock. The party came in two delegations, the first being about six hundred workingmen employed at the La Belle Iron, Steel and Tin Works. The second and larger section arrived about an hour later. In the La Belle delegation were many tin badges and banners, on which were the words "1896. La Belle Iron, Steel and Tin Works." One of these banners was presented to Major McKinley by the workingmen, and when he appeared on his doorstep three hearty cheers were given for him. Hon. WILLIAM C. CURTIS, a member of the West Virginia House of Delegates, stepped forward and congratulated Major McKinley, as follows:

"Mr. PRESIDENT: If there has ever been a nominee of any political party in the history of this country that had a cinch upon that title, you are certainly the man, and as Mr. President I hail you in advance. I have the honor and the pleasure of introducing to you this delegation of iron, steel and tin plate workers of the La Belle Mills of Wheeling, W. Va. (Cheers.) In this delegation we have the president of the mill, the directors, the managers and the workingmen. (Applause.) We have come, irrespective of party affiliation, to do honor to the man by whose instrumentality it was made possible for that mill to manufacture tin plate. Under the bright influence of that law over $100,000 has been expended on the mill, giving it a capacity to turn out thirty tons of tin plate per day. (Loud applause.) Notwithstanding the fact that the enemies of protection told us that we could not manufacture tin plate in this country, yet within four years' time nearly two hundred tin mills have been established with a capital of $9,000,000, employing 12,000 hands, and paying them as wages $8,000,000 per year. Permit me, in conclusion, to present you with this banner made of McKinley tin at the La Belle Mills, and I want to say that I am instructed to pledge to you the enthusiastic support of this delegation from now until the sun sets on the evening of November third, next." (Loud applause.)

Major McKinley's Response.

When the cheering had subsided, Major McKinley replied:

"Mr. CURTIS AND WORKINGMEN OF WHEELING: I beg to thank this great assembly for the generous message of good will and congratulations which you have brought me from the Little Mountain State. There is no tribute greater, there is no tribute that should be dearer to any man, than to have it said, as you have been kind enough to say to me, that he had contributed in the smallest degree to the establishment of an industry new in the United States, which gave additional employment to American labor and brought greater comfort to American homes. I shall long cherish, my fellow citizens, these kindly words, and this demonstration which comes from the workingmen of Wheeling, irrespective of party. I can not misunderstand —nobody can misunderstand—the meaning of these demonstrations on the part of the workingmen. Those who have come here this afternoon, and those

14

who were here this morning, have made their purpose plain and distinct. They mean just one thing; and that is: That in the mind of every American workingman is the thought that this great American doctrine of protection is associated with wages and work, and linked with home, family, country, and prosperity. That, my fellow citizens, is what all these great manifestations signify. They mean that the people of this country want an industrial policy that is for America and Americans. (Loud and continuous applause.) They mean that they intend to return to that policy which lies at the foundation of our National prosperity, which is the safest prop to the National Treasury, and the bulwark of our industrial independence and financial honor. I thank you, workingmen of Wheeling, for this friendly call. I thank you heartily for the kind words you have spoken; I wish you all a safe return home, and I wish for you, and my countrymen everywhere, a speedy return to the happier and better days we used to have." (Great cheering.)

Three-quarters of an hour after the LaBelle delegation had arrived, the second section reached the McKinley residence. It was composed of citizens of Wheeling and members of the Ohio County Republican Club, who created great enthusiasm by their fine appearance. Capt. B. B. Dovener, Member of Congress from the Wheeling district, spoke for the visitors as follows:

"Major McKinley: I have an honor that I appreciate as the spokesman of a Club that represents true Republicanism in our State, a Republicanism that has come up through great tribulation to fight the battles of freedom and the principles of the Republican party. To-day is the anniversary of the birth of West Virginia. I made your acquaintance amid the mountains of our State when we were struggling for the second baptism of liberty and independence in this country. Since that time, thirty-three years ago, we have placed the star representing our State in the firmament of the Union, as bright, we believe, as any that decorates the blue field of our country. These people here are mountaineers of West Virginia, whose Republicanism is as grand as their hills. We bring to you on behalf of the loyal Republicans of our State, from the mountains and the valleys, a glad greeting of congratulation, and know that we shall see you elected President of the United States of America." (Loud cheers.)

Major McKinley's Response.

"Capt. Dovener and My Fellow Citizens of Wheeling: I have been visiting Wheeling for a good many years, and I am glad to have you at last return my frequent calls. (Laughter and applause.) Upon every occasion that I have visited your city and State it was to carry the banner of the Republican party and speak for its immortal principles. I remember having gone through the State in 1894, when the Little Mountain State was transferred from the ranks of our opponents to the columns of the Republican party. (Applause.) I have not seen you since, and therefore take this occasion to congratulate you upon that splendid victory. You put four Republican Representatives in the National House at Washington, and sent that statesman, Stephen B. Elkins, to the Senate (loud cheers) and thus added five more votes to the Republican strength in the great parliamentary bodies of the country. Am I not right in saying, my fellow citizens, that you have come to stay with us? (Loud cries of 'Yes.') That's what you did two years ago, and you mean to keep on doing so, I confidently believe, until the great Republican

15

party shall be brought back into power in every branch of the Federal Government, and until we have returned to that glorious prosperity from which we ran away about four years ago. (Laughter and applause.) I recall with feelings of emotion the reference made by your Congressman, and my friend, Captain DOVENER, to our first meeting over in the Kanawha Valley. We were then in the midst of war; the Southern States, or some of them, were in active rebellion against the Federal Union. Thirty-three years have gone by; the war is long since over, and its glories now belong to the vanquished as well as victors. The settlement sealed at Appomattox is the common heritage of all Americans, and to-day we only know the North and South as geographical divisions. We are all one in devotion to the Union and the flag, and one in striving to make the Nation more glorious than ever before. (Cheers.) I thank you for this call and will be glad to take by the hand each and every one of you. (Applause.)

When Major McKINLEY concluded one of the members of the delegation presented a huge bouquet of roses to Mrs. McKINLEY from the Ohio County Republican Club of Wheeling. He accepted the gift in behalf of Mrs. McKINLEY, with a bow of thanks. The entire delegation then filed past and shook hands with much pleasure and hilarity on part of the enthusiastic Virginia Republicans.

ZANESVILLE SENDS A LARGE DELEGATION.

The demonstrations in honor of Major McKINLEY were resumed Monday afternoon, June 22nd, and by evening were in full force and as joyous as ever. An immense delegation from Zanesville and Dresden arrived over the C., C. and S. Railway at seven o'clock, filling ten coaches. They proceeded at once to Major McKINLEY'S residence; here Hon. HENRY C. VAN VORHS, Member of Congress from the Zanesville district, spoke for the visitors, as follows:

"Major McKINLEY: The people of Muskingum County, the Boys in Blue, the Foraker Club, the McKinley Club, the Young Men's McKinley Club and the Dresden Republican Club are here to congratulate you and the country upon your nomination for the highest office within the gift of the American people. We congratulate you and rejoice with the people of this Nation upon your nomination, because we are assured that it will bring to and end great commercial and industrial depression, and insure protection to our industries, and maintain the honor of our Government. I have the honor, fellow citizens, and it is a great pleasure as well, to introduce to you, the visiting delegations from Muskingum County—Major WILLIAM McKINLEY, the next President of the United States." (Long continued applause.)

Major McKinley's Response.

When the applause had subsided, Major McKINLEY said:

"Mr. VAN VORHS AND MY FELLOW CITIZENS OF MUSKINGUM COUNTY: It appears to me that I have heard those voices before. (A voice, 'That's right.' Laughter and applause.) I am very glad to meet my fellow citizens of Muskingum County. I have many times been greeted by great audiences in the city of Zanesville, but this is the first opportunity I have had to welcome you to my own home. I give you warm and cordial greeting. We have had some experience in the last three years and a half. Experience has superceded prophecy, and cold facts take the place of prediction. We all know more than we knew then, and are ready and anxious to get back a period like that of 1892, when this country was enjoying its highest prosperity with the greatest domestic trade it ever had, and the largest foreign trade ever known with the nations of the world. (Applause.) We want to get back the old policy, my fellow citizens, which will give to labor work and wages, and to agriculture a home market and the good foreign market which was opened up by the reciprocity legislation of the Republican party. We have come to appreciate that protective tariffs are better than idleness, and that wise tariff legislation is more business like than debts and deficiencies, and to feel that the sooner we change the policy which increases the debts of the Government to that of paying as we go, the sooner we will reach individual and National prosperity. And, my countrymen, there is another thing the people are determined upon, and that is that a full day's work must be paid in full dollars. (Cries of 'Good' and loud cheers.) I thank Congressman VAN VOORHIS, and through him all the Clubs of every name, for they are all Republicans this year, (Laughter and shouting), for this cordial visit and promise of support. I will be glad to meet each of you personally and grasp you by the hand." (Tremendous cheers.)

THE CALL OF THE MICHIGAN REPUBLICAN EDITORS.

The Michigan Republican Editorial Association, comprising the editors and proprietors of the leading daily and weekly papers in that State, arrived in Canton on the 1:05 o'clock C., C. & S. train, Wednesday afternoon, June 24th. They came direct from Jackson, Michigan, where they were in session all day Tuesday. While in convention assembled they adopted a resolution by a unanimous vote endorsing the Republican National platform and the nomination of WILLIAM McKINLEY for President. It was then decided to take a trip to Canton and meet the Nation's choice for President, personally. They left Detroit at eleven o'clock by boat to Cleveland, thence to Canton in a special C., C. and S. coach. The party included President F. R. GILSON and wife, editor of the Benton Harbor Palladium ; Secretary W. R. COOK and wife, editor Hastings Banner ; Treasurer Mrs. T. S. APPLEGATE, editor of the Adrian Times and Expositor ; L. A. SHERMAN and wife, of the Port Huron Times ; L. E. SLUSSER, Marcellus Herald ; E. B. DANA, Muskegon Chronicle ; W. E. HOLT, Bellevue Gazette ; DON HENDERSON, Allegan Journal ; C. C. SWENBERG, Grand Rapids Herald ; E. J. MARCH, Hillsdale Leader ; A. L. BEMIS, Carson City Gazette ; E. O. DEWEY and wife, Owasso Times ; C. L. BRECON, Grand Haven Daily News ; J. C. JONES and F. WARD, Hillsdale Standard ; C. S. BROWN, Banner Publishing Co., Hastings ; GEORGE BARNES, Livingston County Republican, Howell ; J. H. KIDD and wife, Daily Sentinel, Iona ; JAMES O'DONNELL, editor of the Daily Citizen, Jackson ; L. MERCHANT, of the St. Joseph Herald ; W. J. HUNSAKER, manager of the Detroit Journal ; E. L. BATES, Pentwater News ; L. P. BISSELL, Eaton Country Republican ; FRED SLOCUM and wife, Tuscola County Advertiser, Cairo ; C. J. MOORE and wife, of the Battle Creek Daily Journal ; B. J. LOWREY, editor Howard City Record ; L. M. SELLERS, Cedar Springs Clipper ; GEORGE E. GILLIAM, Hornsville Record ; GEORGE DEWEY, Jr., Owosso Times ; ROY GILSON, Benton Harbor, H. G. BARNUM and wife, and E. G. SPALDING and wife, Port Huron Publishing Co. ; C. A. BAXTER, of Detroit, Member of the National

17

Committee of the Republican League, and W. H. Sweet, of Ypsilanti. The visitors were conducted to the McKinley residence and personally received by Major and Mrs. McKinley. On behalf of the visitors, ex-Congressman O'Donnel introduced President Gilson, who said:

"Major McKinley: We have come to your home to add our voices to the great chorus of congratulations that come to you from all over the Nation. We come from Michigan, a State that has vast agricultural and commercial interests, all to be benefitted through your influence—a State now solidly Republican. We come from a profession which has done much in the past to educate the people along the line of material development, that is devoted to the American flag, the American farm, the American factory, and the American fireside. We owe much to you as business men and business women. The largest cities in our State are represented here—Detroit and Grand Rapids—as well as a number of the larger towns. We came so soon after the nomination that we had not time to gather in our hosts, so that our party is but a small part of what it would otherwise have been."

Major McKinley's Response.

"Mr. Gilson and Ladies and Gentlemen: I count it a very great honor, as well as a very great pleasure, to receive this visit from the Republican editors of the State of Michigan. I have noted for many years the ability of the press of your State, I have noted that the Republican press of Michigan has never faltered in its loyalty to Republican principles, but under all circumstances has been faithful to the Republican cause. Nor have I permitted to pass unobserved the very friendly personal spirit which has been shown me for long years by the Republican editors of your State; during the discussions preceding the Republican National Convention, your partiality was so strongly marked, and so generous, that I can not now forbear to thank you. When your great State, through its representatives at St. Louis spoke, it spoke unitedly, showing that the Republican press and the people of Michigan this year were of one mind. The power which you, ladies and gentlemen, exercise on the destinies of the country can not be over estimated. You not only register public opinion, but you have much to do with making and influencing public opinion, and in a government like ours, where public opinion lies at the foundation, and is supreme to government, the press is, indeed, mighty in its power. A partisan press, too, is indispensable in a government like ours. As long as we have parties we must have party newspapers, and it is very gratifying to me to know that to-day the Republican party never had such strength and support as it is receiving from the press of the United States. Its aims, its purposes, and its principles are nearer and dearer to Republicans than ever before, and I believe that they are nearer and dearer to the great masses of our countrymen, considered independent of past party affiliations, than they have ever been in the past, and that those principles never so well deserved the support of the press as now. (Applause.) In this great National contest you will have very much to do with the result, and I am sure the editors of the State of Michigan, the Republican editors, can be counted upon to give to those great principles of our party that so closely affect the prosperity of the country their best efforts this year, as they have ever done in the years of the past. It has given both Mrs. McKinley and myself genuine pleasure to have you in our home. We bid you all welcome." (Applause.)

18

A UNIQUE AND ELEGANT HOME RECEPTION.

The women of Canton, prompted by their great esteem for Major and Mrs. McKinley, gave them an unique and elegant reception at the Jacob Miller homestead, West Tuscarawas Street, on Friday afternoon, June 26th. It had long been unoccupied but the good women of Canton had most beautifully refurnished and decorated it, in honor of the occasion. Here gathered several thousands of the women of Canton and Stark County to testify their respect and reverence for Major and Mrs. McKinley, and his venerable mother, Mrs. William McKinley, Sr. They crowded the Miller homestead, and the spacious grounds surrounding it; the reception began at 3:00 o'clock, and for the next two hours thousands of women paid their respects to their distinguished guests of honor. At the conclusion of the reception, Mrs. Alice D. Jones, of Canton, spoke for the assembled thousands:

"Mother and Wife of William McKinley: You know the import of this meeting. We, the women of Canton and Stark County, would show honor to the two women nearest and dearest to the man to whom not only Canton but the entire Nation is paying homage. He is bound to you by ties even closer than those which bind him to his country and we believe he will say with us that the better part of him is of your making. The path which we now see so plainly leading to the White House had its beginning within the doorway of the little frame house in Niles. There the wisdom of a father and the loving guidance of a mother, laid the foundation of the young boy's life, the justice, the sagacity, and the charity of which characterize the statesman of to-day. Ah, Mother, the little hands you guided then have been growing stronger as your own have grown more feeble! Life's discipline of calm and storm has left its marks upon your boy's face, but the necessary lessons and songs are still remembered, and the touch of your aged hands upon them to-day is a motive power for good, so pure, so limitless in its reach, that only balances unseen can estimate its worth. Mrs. McKinley, over twenty-five years ago you prophesied Canton's future pride in Canton's young attorney. You plighted to him your girlish faith and within the old Presbyterian church you linked your life with his. Canton has been proud of him for many years, and Canton has been proud of you. Governor McKinley's every act to-day bears upon it the stamp of his association with a refined, exalted womanhood. So purely womanly is you wifely devotion, so in sympathy with his every interest has your life always been, that were you not a part of it to-day we believe like Lafayette, he would exclaim, in the bitterness of his heart, "She was so one with me, that life seems robbed of half its power without her!" Proud as we are of our statesman, we boast in wife's and mother's part in giving to us one in whom we can all safely trust. Women such as you have given our Nation in the past her noblest bravest sons. John Quincy Adams owed his greatness to his mother; Washington consulted his mother; Lucy Webb Hayes was her husband's truest helper; Jackson deferred to the opinions of his idolized wife; and the name of Ida Saxton McKinley will ever be associated with the fame of her illustrious husband. Fourteen years ago on the Sunday following his nomination, James A. Garfield walked into the old home church, bearing on his arm his aged mother, and on last Sabbath morning into the church of his early faith walked our future President, and with him walked his mother. With home anchorage such as this, we women have no fears that under the coming Administration hearth-fires will burn dimmer or counting-rooms be closed. Men may deal with questions of tariff and finance and political policy; we women believe the importance of pure living is higher than all and are satisfied that if you are called to preside over the destinies of the Nation, we shall have a man at the head with a character so pure and a record so untarnished that any mother here to-day would feel proud to know that the footsteps of their little boys were parallel with his. Major and Mrs. McKinley, in giving you to the Nation, we do not feel that we are losing you. Too many ties, sacred and tender, will bring you back to Canton. There are pleasant friendships here, there are deeper loves, there are homes on Market and West Tuscarawas, and, out in Westlawn, there are tiny graves, and larger ones, which will ever make Canton a Mecca for your returning feet. In this your hour of triumph, and ours of pride, when to you and yours we extend the congratulations of your townswomen we can not refrain from paying tribute to one, who, bearing also the name of McKinley, will be remembered in Canton as long as those who came in contact with her have the powers of memory. Anna McKinley possessed that latent power, that force of character, that winning charm and gracious tact, which made her queenly among women, and which, had she been a man, would have made her second, not even to her honored brother, William McKinley. No richer benison can we ask for you, than where, with wider reach, perchance than hers, your hands may guide and govern." (Applause.)

Major McKinley's Response.

Fully 6,000 of the women of Canton and Stark County took part in this memorable reception. Major McKinley thanked the great assemblage for the honor done his wife and mother, but did not continue his remarks beyond a brief acknowledgment. He said:

"Mrs. Jones and Women of Canton: I am sure that both my wife and mother would have me express their warm appreciation of the gracious words you have spoken, and I assure you that no honor can ever come to me that I will esteem more highly than this loving tribute that you have paid to those who are so near and dear to me. In a single word I wish to add that I feel no higher commendation can be paid to any man than to have the approval of the good women, mothers, wives, sisters, friends, of the city in which he lives. It will give my wife and mother both the greatest pleasure to meet you all personally. Again, I thank you." (Applause.)

NORWALK AND HURON COUNTY.

The Young Men's Republican Club, the Huron County Republican Committee and other citizens of Norwalk, Ohio, arrived in Canton at seven o'clock Friday evening, June 26th, to extend their congratulations and proffer their support to Major McKinley. The delegation came via the Wheeling and Lake Erie Railroad to Massillon and thence to Canton on the Interurban Electric Railway, a journey of about one hundred miles. It was headed by the A. B. Chase Band and accompanied by a Colored Glee Club. Judge Thomas called the visitors to order, and in a few remarks introduced Hon. Lewis C. Laylin, ex-Speaker of the House of Representatives, who said:

"Major McKinley: The Young Men's Republican Club of Norwalk, members of the Huron County Central Committee, and many others, ask me to convey to you their congratulations upon your nomination for President. Forty years ago, when the Republican party was organized, a majority of the voters of Huron County gave it their allegiance as the party of freedom, and from then until the present hour, not a single Democrat has been elected to a county office in old Huron. It is always ready with a Republican majority. In every campaign it contributes to the party's victories, victories which have given us such immortal statesmen as LINCOLN, GRANT, HAYES, GARFIELD and HARRISON. When the Democratic party came into power three years ago, when the matchless tariff measure which bears your honored name was stricken from the statute books, our people, in common with many thousand more Republicans of this and other States, resolved upon your leadership in the contest of 1896. We are here at your home now to bring our hearty greetings and to congratulate the country on the dawn of the brighter day that will be ushered in by your election. Accept our greetings and the assurance of our abiding confidence in your great triumph in November next." (Applause.)

Major McKinley's Response.

"SPEAKER LAYLIN AND MY FELLOW CITIZENS OF HURON COUNTY: It gives me great pleasure to meet you, and I am grateful to your spokesman, who has been my friend for many years, for the generous words he has spoken, in the expression of your respect and good will. I recall that Huron County was one of the counties of this State that gave its support to JOHN C. FREMONT, our first candidate for President of the United States, and in all the eventful years that have followed has steadily kept the faith in every contest. This is creditable to both the patriotism and intelligence of her people, for no man anywhere throughout the country doubts where the Republican party stood in times past nor where it stands to-day. It stands for a re-united and prosperous country; it stands for the American factory, the American farm, the American fireside, for American labor, American wages and American thrift throughout every part of our much loved land. It stands for a protective tariff which protects every American interest; it stands for reciprocity that reciprocates—that gets something for what we give, from the nations of the world. It stands for the reciprocity of BLAINE and of HARRISON and the great Republican party. It stands now, as it has always stood, and always will stand, for sound money with which to measure the exchanges of the people, for a dollar that is not only good at home, but good in every market place of the world. It is with these principles emblazoned on its banners this year of 1896 that it appeals to the deliberate judgment of the American people. LINCOLN used to say, "there is no better hope in the world than this," and to such a tribunal we, therefore, feel that we can confidently submit our aims and purposes." (Great and long continued applause.)

THE CANTON RATIFICATION AND PARADE.

Canton was again the Mecca of thousands of people on Saturday, June 27th. The threatening weather did not prevent their coming to Major McKinley's home city to assist the great crowd from Cleveland in ratifying his nomination. The exercises were under the auspices of the Tippecanoe Club, one of the

21

most famous Republican clubs in the country, but there were a score or more of other large delegations from as many towns within a radius of a hundred miles of Canton. Both at the speaking in the afternoon, at the corner of Third Street and Cleveland Avenue, where a crowd collected filling the entire open square, and as the immense parade passed the reviewing stand in front of Major McKinley's residence at night, the enthusiasm was unbounded. Judge WILLIAM R. DAY, of Canton, presided at the meeting in the park, and strong speeches were made by General CHARLES H. GROSVENOR, of Athens, Ohio, Hon. CHARLES EMORY SMITH, the distinguished journalist of Philadelphia, Hon. JAMES H. HOYT, of Cleveland, Hon. ROBERT W. TAYLER, of Lisbon, and Mr. H. W. WOLCOTT, President of the Tippecanoe Club, of Cleveland. The great feature of the speaking exercises, however, was the ovation given to Major McKinley, as he came upon the rostrum to acknowledge the demonstrations in his honor. He spoke as follows:

Major McKinley's Response.

"MY FELLOW CITIZENS: I thank you for this magnificent demonstration; I think I know just what it means. It is in no sense personal—but it is the assurance of the interest which you feel in the great questions that are to be considered in this eventful campaign, and settled by the American people at the November election. It means, my fellow citizens, that you are attached by every tie of fealty and affection to the great fundamental doctrines of the Republican party. It means that you intend by your votes to write into public law, to place permanently upon our statute books, what you believe to be for the best interests of all the American people. (Loud and continuous applause.) Republican principles do not perish. They have not suffered by defeat. They have not been dimmed by their temporary rejection by the people. They are brighter and more glorious to-day than ever before. (Cries of 'Good,' and 'That's right.') They are doubly dear to every American heart. (Loud applause. Their defeat before the American people has never brought good to any American interest, (A voice, 'Not one') but their triumph has always brought many and far-reaching advantages to the American people. (Applause.) My fellow citizens, these principles are to be tried before you this year—what will your answer be in November? (A voice, 'The election of McKinley!' tremendous cheering lasting several moments before the Major could resume his speech.) What are these principles, my fellow citizens? A protective tariff that takes care of every American interest, and serves the highest good of American labor (Great cheering.) A tariff that insists that our work shall be done at home and not abroad. (Loud yelling and applause.) A reciprocity, that, while seeking out the world's markets for our surplus products, will never yield up a single day's work that belongs to the American workingman. (Vociferous cheering.) Honest money, a dollar as sound as the Government, and as untarnished as its flag. (Loud cheers.) A dollar that is as good in the hands of the farmer and the workingman, as in the hands of the manufacturer or the capitalist. (Cheers.) These great principles emblazoned as they are upon the banners of the Republican party will insure a sweeping triumph—so that the third day of November next, will, as I firmly believe, bring sweet messages of promise and happiness to every American home and fireside throughout this broad land. (Continuous cheers.) I thank you, my fellow citizens, for this manifestation of your good will. I am glad to welcome you to this city—a city near and dear to me by every tie of affection—a city to which I owe much. We are all proud to have you here to-day, and my advice to the Mayor is to have the census taken at once." (Laughter and renewed applause."

APOLLO (PENNSYLVANIA) REPUBLICAN CLUB.

Just after the Ratification meeting on Market Square had closed, the members of the Apollo (Pennsylvania) Republican Club, who had arrived by a special train too late to hear the speeches there, called upon Major McKINLEY at his residence, and prevailed upon him to say "just a word" from the reviewing stand on his lawn. He said:

Major McKinley's Response.

"GENTLEMEN OF THE APOLLO REPUBLICAN CLUB: I assure you I very cordially appreciate the courtesy and compliment of this call; I appreciate it the more because I know it means that you have traveled this long distance that you might give evidence of the interest you feel in the questions that are engaging public attention and which the people will determine later on. I congratulate your busy little manufacturing city upon the progress and prosperity it has had, and I trust that in the future you will have still greater prosperity.

Some one has said that 'we are a nation of working people, and born busy.' Well, we have been, and will be again; and that policy, under which for more than thirty years we enjoyed exceptional advantages and prosperity shall be again restored to this country. I thank you all for the compliment of this call and bid you good afternoon." (Tremendous applause and three cheers.)

SENATOR THURSTON'S NOTIFICATION ADDRESS.

On Monday, June 29th, the Presidential Notification Committee appointed by the St. Louis Convention called upon Major McKINLEY, at his home in Canton, to formally apprise him of his nomination as the Republican candidate for President in 1896. Hon. JOHN M. THURSTON, of Nebraska, Permanent Chairman of the National Convention, spoke for the Committee. He said:

"Major McKINLEY: We are here to perform the pleasant duty assigned us by the Republican National Convention, recently assembled in St. Louis, that of formally notifying you of your nomination as the candidate of the Republican party for President of the United States. We respectfully request your acceptance of this nomination and your approval of the declaration of principles adopted by the Convention. We assure you that you are the unanimous choice of a united party, and that your candidacy will be immediately accepted by the country as an absolute guaranty of Republican success. Your nomination has been made in obedience to a popular demand whose universality and spontaneity attest the affection and confidence of the plain people of the United States. By common consent you are their champion. Their mighty uprising in your behalf emphasizes the sincerity of their conversion to the cardinal principles of Protection and Reciprocity as best exemplified in that splendid Congressional Act which justly bears your name. Under it this Nation advanced to the very culmination of a prosperity far surpassing that of all other peoples and all other times; a prosperity shared in by all sections, all interests and all classes; by capital and labor; by producer and consumer; a prosperity so happily in harmony with the genius of popular government that its choicest blessings were most widely distributed among the lowliest toilers and humblest homes. In 1892, your countrymen, unmindful of your solemn warnings, returned that party to power which reiterated its ever-lasting opposition to a protective tariff and demanded the repeal of the McKinley Act. They sowed the wind. They reaped the whirlwind. The sufferings and losses and disasters to the American people from four years of Democratic tariff, are vastly greater than those which came to them from four years of civil war. Out of it all great good remains. Those who scorned your counsels speedily witnessed the fulfillment of your prophesies, and even as the scourged and repentant Israelites abjured their stupid idols and resumed unquestioning allegiance to Moses and Moses' God, so now your countrymen, shamed of their errors, turn to you and to those glorious principles for which you stand, in the full belief that your candidacy and the Republican platform mean that the end of the wilderness has come and the promised land of American prosperity is again to them an assured inheritance. But your nom-ination means more than the endorsement of a protective tariff, of reciprocity of sound money and of honest finance, for all of which you have so steadfastly stood. It means an endorsement of your heroic youth; your faithful years of arduous public service; your sterling patriotism; your starlwart Americanism; your Christian character, and the purity, fidelity and simplicity of your private life. In all these things you are the typical American; for all these things you are the chosen leader of the people. God give you strength to so bear the honors and meet the duties of that great office for which you are now nominat-ed and to which you will be elected, that your administration will enhance the dignity and power and glory of this Republic, and secure the safety, welfare and happiness of its liberty-loving people." (Great applause.)

Major McKinley's Response.

"Senator Thurston and Gentlemen of the Notification Committee of the Republican National Convention: To be selected as their Presidential candidate by a great party convention, representing so vast a number of the people of the United States, is a most distinguished honor, for which I would not conceal my high appreciation, although deeply sensible of the great responsibilities of the trust, and my inability to bear them without the gener-ous and constant support of my fellow countrymen. Great as is the honor conferred, equally arduous and important is the duty imposed, and in accept-ing the one I assume the other, relying upon the patriotic devotion of the people to the best interests of our beloved country, and the sustaining care and aid of Him without whose support all we do is empty and vain. Should the people ratify the choice of the great Convention for which you speak, my only aim will be to promote the public good, which in America is always the good of the greatest number, the honor of our country, and the welfare of the people. The questions to be settled in the National contest this year are as serious and important as any of the great governmental problems that have confronted us in the past quarter of a century. They command our sober judgment, and a settlement free from partisan prejudice and passion, beneficial to our selves and befitting the honor and grandeur of the Republic. They touch every interest of our common country. Our industrial supremacy, our productive capacity, our business and commercial prosperity, our labor and its rewards, our National credit and currency, our proud financial honor, and our splendid free citizenship—the birthright of every American— are all involved in the pending campaign, and thus every home in the land is directly and intimately connected with their proper settlement. Great are the issues involved in the coming election, and eager and earnest the people for their right determination. Our domestic trade must be won back, and our idle working people employed in gainful occupations at American wages. Our home market must be restored to its proud rank of first in the world, and our foreign trade, so precipitately cut off by adverse National legislation, reopened on fair and equitable terms for our surplus agricultural and manufacturing products. Protection and Reciprocity, twin measures of a true American policy, should again command the earnest encouragement of the Government at Washington. Public confidence must be resumed, and the skill, the energy and the capital of our country find ample employment at home, sustained, encouraged and defended against the unequal competition and serious disadvantages with which they are now contending. (Applause.)

"The Government of the United States must raise enough money to meet both its current expenses and increasing needs. Its revenues should be so raised as to protect the material interests of our people, with the lightest possible drain upon their resources, and maintain that high standard of civilization which has distinguished our country for more than a century of its existence. The income of the Government, I repeat, should equal its necessary and proper expenditures. A failure to pursue this policy has compelled the Government to borrow money in a time of peace to sustain its credit and pay its daily expenses. This policy should be reversed, and that, too, as speedily as possible. It must be apparent to all, regardless of past party ties or affiliations, that it is our paramount duty to provide adequate revenue for the expenditures of the Government, economically and prudently administered. This the Republican party has heretofore done, and this I confidently believe it will do in the future, when the party is again entrusted with power in the legislative and executive branches of our Government. The National credit, which has thus far fortunately resisted every assault upon it, must and will be upheld and strengthened. If sufficient revenues are provided for the support of the Government, there will be no necessity for borrowing money and increasing the public debt. The complaint of the people is not against the Administration for borrowing money and issuing bonds to preserve the credit of the country, but against the ruinous policy which has made this necessary. It is but an incident, and a necessary one, to the policy which has been inaugurated. The inevitable effect of such a policy is seen in the deficiency of the United States Treasury, except as it is replenished by loans, and in the distress of the people who are suffering because of the scant demand for either their labor or the products of their labor. Here is the fundamental trouble, the remedy for which is Republican opportunity and duty. During all the years of Republican control following resumption, there was a steady reduction of the public debt, while the gold reserve was sacredly maintained, and our currency and credit preserved without depreciation, taint or suspicion. If we would restore this policy, that brought us unexampled prosperity for more than thirty years under the most trying conditions ever known in this country, the policy by which we made and bought more goods at home and sold more abroad, the trade balance would be quickly turned in our favor, and gold would come to us and not go from us in the settlement of all such balances in the future. (Cheers.)

"The party that supplied by legislation the vast revenues for the conduct of our greatest war; that promptly restored the credit of the country at its close; that from its abundant revenues paid off a large share of the debt incurred in this war, and that resumed specie payments and placed our paper currency upon a sound and enduring basis, can be safely trusted to preserve both our credit and currency, with honor, stability and inviolability. The American people hold the financial honor of our Government as sacred as our flag, and can be relied upon to guard it with the same sleepless vigilance. They hold its preservation above party fealty, and have often demonstrated that party ties avail nothing when the spotless credit of our country is threatened. The money of the United States, and every kind or form of it, whether of paper, silver or gold, must be as good as the best in the world. It must not only be current at its full face value at home, but it must be counted at par in any and every commercial center of the globe. The sagacious and far-seeing policy of the great men who founded our Government; the teachings and acts of the wisest financiers at every stage in our history; the steadfast faith and splendid achievements of the great party to which we belong, and the genius and integrity of our people have always demanded this, and will ever maintain it. The dollar paid to the farmer, the wage-earner, and the pensioner must continue forever equal in purchasing and debt-paying power to the dollar paid to any Government creditor. (Great applause.)

"The contest this year will not be waged upon lines of theory and speculation, but in the light of severe practical experience and new and dearly acquired knowledge. The great body of our citizens know what they want, and that they intend to have. They know for what the Republican party stands and what its return to power means to them. They realize that the Republican party believes that our work should be done at home and not abroad, and everywhere proclaim their devotion to the principles of a protective tariff, which, while supplying adequate revenues for the Government, will restore American production, and serve the best interests of American labor and development. Our appeal, therefore, is not to a false philosophy, or vain theorists, but to the masses of the American people, the plain, practical people, whom Lincoln loved and trusted, and whom the Republican party has always faithfully striven to serve. (Applause.)

" The Platform adopted by the Republican National Convention has received my careful consideration and has my unqualified approval. It is a matter of gratification to me, as I am sure it must be to you and Republicans everywhere, and to all our people, that the expressions of its declaration of principles are so direct, clear and emphatic. They are too plain and positive to leave any chance for doubt or question as to their purport and meaning. But you will not expect me to discuss its provisions at length, or in any detail, at this time. It will, however, be my duty and pleasure at some future day to make to you, and through you to the great party you represent, a more formal acceptance of the nomination tendered me.

"No one could be more profoundly grateful than I am for the manifestations of public confidence of which you have so eloquently spoken. It shall be my aim to attest this appreciation by an unsparing devotion to what I esteem the best interests of the people, and in this work I ask the counsel and support of you, gentlemen, and of every other friend of the country. The generous expressions with which you, sir, convey the official notice of my nomination are highly appreciated, and as fully reciprocated, and I thank you, and your associates of the Notification Committee, and the great party and convention at whose instance you come, for the high and exceptional distinction bestowed upon me." (Great applause, and "three cheers for our next President."

The Notification Committee consisted of the following gentlemen: Alabama, CHARLES D. ALEXANDER, Attalla; Alaska, C. S. JOHNSON, Juneau; Arizona, JOHN W. DORRINGTON, Yuma; Arkansas, HENRY M. COOPER, Little Rock, represented by Colonel H. L. REMMEL, Newport; California, FRANK A. MILLER, Riverside; Connecticut, GEORGE E. SYKES, Rockville; Delaware, HENRY G. MORSE, Wilmington; Florida, DENNIS EAGAN, Jacksonville; Georgia, MONROE E. MORTON, (colored), Athens; Illinois, CHARLES H. DEERE, Moline; Indiana, HIRAM BROWNLEE, Marion; Indian Territory, JOSEPH R. FOLTZ, South McAlister; Iowa, CALVIN MANNING, Ottumwa; Kansas, NATHANIEL BARNES, Kansas City; Kentucky, JOHN P. McCARTNEY, Flemingsburg; Louisiana, WALTER L. COHEN, (colored), New Orleans; Maine, GEORGE P. WESTCOTT, Portland, represented by Hon. CHARLES E. TOWNSEND, Brunswick; Maryland, WILLIAM F. AIRY, Baltimore; Massachusetts, MARTIN V. B. JEFFERSON, Worcester; Michigan, THOMAS J. O'BRIEN, Grand Rapids; Minnesota, MONROE NICHOLS, Duluth; Mississippi, W. D. FRAZEE, West Point; Missouri, T. H. HAUGHAWOUT, Carthage; Nebraska, JOHN T. BRESSLER, Wayne; Nevada, JOHN B. OVERTON, Virginia City; New Hampshire, WILLIAM D. SAWYER, Dover; New Jersey, FERDINAND W. ROEBLING, Trenton; New Mexico, PEDRO PEREA, Bernalillo, represented by Captain JACK CRAWFORD, "the Poet Scout," Santa Fe; New York, FRANK HISCOCK, Saratoga; North Carolina, CLAUDE M. BERNARD, Greenville; North Dakota, C. M. JOHNSON, Dwight; Ohio, MARCUS A. HANNA, Cleveland; Oklahoma, JOHN A. BUCKLES, Enid; Oregon, CHARLES B. HILTON, The Dalles; Pennsylvania, THEODORE L. FLOOD, Meadville; Rhode Island, JOHN C. SANBORN, Newport; South Carolina, E. H. DEES, (colored), Darlington, South Dakota, WALTER E. SMEAD, Lead City; Tennessee, ERNEST CALDWELL, Shelbyville; Texas, J. W. BUTLER, Tyler; Utah, LINDSAY R. ROGERS, Ogden; Vermont, JAMES W. BROCK, Montpelier, represented by Judge H. A. HUSE, Burlington; Virginia, J. S. BROWNING, Pocahontas; Washington, HENY L. WILSON, Spokane; West Virginia, W. NEWTON LYNCH, Martinsburg; Wisconsin, M. C. RING, Neillsville; Wyoming, HENRY J. NICKERSON, Lander. Hon. CHARLES W. FAIRBANKS, of Indianapolis, Temporary Chairman of the National Convention, was also present, and spoke at the notification meeting. The notification exercises were held at Major McKinley's residence, himself, wife and mother, with other members of the family, appearing on the front porch, from which Senator THURSTON and himself spoke to the Committee, who were seated on camp chairs on the lawn during the entire ceremonies, which were witnessed by thousands of enthusiastic visitors and citizens. At their close a luncheon was served the Committee in a large tent on the lawn in the rear of the residence.

THE CONVENTION GAVEL.

During the notification proceedings Mr. HENRY H. SMITH, of Washington, D. C., formerly a clerk in the House of Representatives, presented Major McKinley with the gavel used in the St. Louis Convention when he was nominated for President. Its history, as described by Mr. SMITH, is as follows:

"Major McKinley: This gavel was presented to the National Convention by Mr. W. H. Bartells, of Carthage, Illinois. It was made from a log taken from the cabin occupied by Abraham Lincoln in 1832 at Salem, Illinois. On one head of the gavel is inscribed on a silver plate the name of the donor and the above stated facts, while on the other on a gold plate, appear the words: 'National Republican Convention, held at St. Louis, Missouri, June 16, 1896, nominating William McKinley for President.' This gavel, which stands as en emblem and type of sturdy Americanism and American homes and industries, was placed in my hands as Assistant Secretary of the Convention, and of the Notification Committee, for presentation to you on this most happy occasion."

Major McKinley's Response.

"Mr. Smith: I thank you for this beautiful gift, and for the courteous terms in which you have conveyed the wishes of the Convention. I am glad to have so valuable a souvenir of the eleventh great National Convention of the Republican party, and am especially grateful for the remembrance on account of the historic associations connecting it with the name of the martyred Lincoln, whose memory is an inspiration to every American." (Applause.)

COLUMBUS CLUBS CONGRATULATE HIM.

While the Committee on Notification were lunching a large delegation from Columbus, Ohio, arrived via the Ft. Wayne Railroad. There were seven coaches in the train bringing the delegation, and included in it were the Buckeye Republican Club, the Columbus Glee Club, and several hundred other citizens, headed by the famous Fourteenth Regiment Band. They marched at once to the McKinley residence where they were presented by Hon. David K. Watson, Member of Congress from the Columbus district, who spoke as follows:

"Major McKinley: The Republicans of the Capital City of this State have come to pay their respects to you as the candidate for President of the United States, nominated at St. Louis by the great Republican party to the highest and greatest office which it is possible for a human being to occupy. During the four years that you were Governor of Ohio you resided among us, and in that time we learned to greatly admire and esteem you personally, and to have unbounded confidence in your future life. The Republican party is entering upon its eleventh great contest for National supremacy. Forty years ago it lost its first battle under the leadership of Fremont, because the States of Pennsylvania and Illinois cast their electoral votes for the Democratic candidate. But those great States have quit that nonsense, and this year their electoral votes will be cast for you. (Loud cheers.) The Republican party won its second and third great contests under the leadership of Lincoln; its fourth and fifth under Grant; its sixth under Hayes; its seventh under Garfield; we lost the eighth under Blaine; won the ninth under Harrison, and lost with him the tenth. But, sir, we know we will win the eleventh under your magnificent leadership. (Loud applause.) In the halls of Congress you were the one great man who always led American thought in the direction of protection to American labor. (Cheers.) You have always stood for a higher American manhood and the development of American character. Your

28

National policy gave American markets to American products at American prices, and to-day, as ever, you still stand for all that is Republican and American. You are to many people, in a peculiar sense, both candidate and platform, and condensed the entire issue of this campaign into a single sentence when you declared at Chicago on Lincoln's birthday, last February, that 'the Republican party stands now, as ever in the past, for an honest dollar and the chance to earn it by honest toil." (Cheers.) The Republicans of Columbus, Ohio, greet you as the next President of this, the great Republic." (Prolonged applause.)

Major McKinley's Response.

"CONGRESSMAN WATSON AND MY FELLOW CITIZENS OF COLUMBUS: You have done me great honor which I highly appreciate, by the call you have made upon me to-day. It is with great pleasure I recall the four years I spent in the Capital City, for that old town became, indeed, very dear to me. I felt through those years that there was not a moment that I did not have the sympathy, the support, the good will, the constant encouragement of the citizens of Columbus, irrespective of political affiliations. No four years of my public service were more agreeable to me, and I shall always cherish their pleasant memories. (Applause.) I thank you, Congressman WATSON, for the gracious words you have spoken personal to myself. I do believe in my country, I believe in its vast resources and capacities, and I believe that it is entirely with the people to say what shall be the possibilities of the future for the United States. LINCOLN said the people never had been appealed to in the right way in vain, and I am sure, in the bright light of his faith, that the people of this country, from ocean to ocean, will stand by those principles and policies that will secure to the United States the greatest prosperity and conserve its highest destiny. (Cheers.) We have present with us, and it gives me great pleasure to present to you, some of the Notification Committee from the Republican National Convention. The first gentleman I desire to present is that illustrious citizen of Nebraska, her great United States Senator, Hon. JOHN M. THURSTON." (Prolonged applause.)

Senator Thurston's Pleasant Response.

"MY FELLOW CITIZENS: It has been a matter of great gratification to me to come here to-day in an official capacity for the purpose of bringing notification to Major McKINLEY that the people of this country had determined that he shall be the next President of the United States. (Loud applause.) We have come to Ohio once again for our candidate, but not merely because Ohio is his native State. WASHINGTON and LINCOLN do not belong to Virginia and Illinois alone, they are part of the priceless inheritance of the American people. Ohio has given birth to GRANT and GARFIELD, HAYES and HARRISON, and, great as any—McKINLEY. (Loud applause.) But we made them Presidents of the United States not because they stood for the State of Ohio, but because they stood for the Nation, as broad as the land and an Americanism as glorious as the flag. (Loud applause.) Four years ago the Democratic party said to the American people, "Give us free trade, and the prosperity of this country will increase." You voted free trade and prosperity receded. They said, "Give us

29

free trade and new industries and factories will open,"——but they closed. They said, "Give us free trade and there will be increased employment for American labor."——but there was increased idl·ness instead. They said. "Give us free trade and wages will rise,"——but they failed to rise. They said, "Give us free trade and business will boom,"——but it busted (Laughter and applause.) To-day in the light of their past experience it is absolutely necessary to abandon their old petition, and they now say, "Give us free silver and all these glorious results will follow." Don't you think in the light of their past repudiation and bankruptcy that you had better have a little collateral security before you accept their new promise of American prosperity? (Loud applause.) The Republican party stands for a dollar on which there shall be an American eagle—but with no feathers dragging in the dust. (Applause.) The Republican party declares that the labor which is to be done for the people of the United States shall be done by the people of the United States and under the glorious old Stars and Stripes. (Cheers.) I thank you for this distinction and for your kindness in listening to me. From now until the campaign closes, I shall go forward from stump to stump not only with boundless enthusiasm for the platform and for the nominees but with the absolute assurance that the American people know what they want and that they are getting it just as fast as they can." (Loud cheers.)

Mr. Hiscock's Happy Reply.

Major McKinley then introduced ex-Senator Frank Hiscock, of Syracuse, New York, who spoke as follows:

"Ladies and Gentlemen: You are here to-day as the immediate friends and neighbors of Major McKinley, the candidate of the Republican party for the Presidency. Your hearts are overflowing with love for him; your judgments approve him and you most heartily endorse the principles for which he has so long labored, and which are now the platform of the Republican party. I came here from the State of New York, representing that State as a member of the Notification Committee to notify him of his nomination, and I say to you that he is as truly in the hearts of the people of the State of New York, as he is in yours. (Loud applause.) I proclaim to you without fear of contradiction, that he is as much approved by the Republicans of the State of New York, and not by their judgments alone, but by those of one-half of the Democratic party of the State of New York also (laughter and applause) as he is by you. This year we had a superabundance of candidates for the Presidency—men justly presented as statesmen of no mean merit. Thomas B. Reed is a great man. (Applause.) New York presented the name of the grand Governor of our State, Levi P. Morton, who was elected by 156,000 majority. (Applause.) Iowa presented the name of William B. Allison, her great statesman. (Applause.) But Ohio presented the name of William McKinley. (Loud yells and applause.) Now I say to you, confidentially, that before Ohio presented his name the people had already in their hearts ratified his nomination. (Laughter and applause.) I have only this to say to you in conclusion: We have our own little difficulties in New York, once in a while. (Laughter and applause.) But while that is true, and while it is a fact that we have as many difficulties and fight as severely over them as the people of any other State in the Union, still in proportion to population, as well as in actual figures,

New York will give a larger majority for WILLIAM McKINLEY next November than Ohio can possibly give him." (Great applause.)

Excellent short speeches were also made of the most enthusiastic character by Hon. CHARLES E. TOWNSEND, of Maine; Dr. THEODORE L. FLOOD, of Pennsylvania, Hon. J. S. BROWNING, of Virginia; Judge J. A. HUSE, of Vermont; Hon. HENRY L. WILSON, of Washington; Hon. CHARLES W. FAIRBANKS, of Indiana; Colonel H. L. REMMEL, of Arkansas; Hon. CALVIN MANNING, of Iowa; Hon. M. V. B. JEFFERSON, of Massachusetts, and Hon. M. A. HANNA, of Ohio, while an original poem was recited by Captain JACK CRAWFORD, of New Mexico. It is safe to say that never on any previous occasion of the kind had there been so great a demonstration; never such indisputable evidences of harmony, enthusiasm, and confidence; never such determination to succeed, and never a more flattering prospect of sweeping success.

THE UNION VETERAN LEGION.

At the conclusion of the speech-making, at the Notification Meeting on June 29th, a committee of soldiers from Columbus, Ohio, waited upon Major McKINLEY and presented him the following interesting memorial:

HEADQUARTERS ENCAMPMENT NO. 78,
 UNION VETERAN LEGION.

COLUMBUS, OHIO, June 23, 1896.

WHEREAS, One of the members of this encampment, in the person of Comrade WILLIAM McKINLEY, has been selected by one of the great political parties as its candidate for President at the coming National election; therefore be it

Resolved by this Encampment, That we congratulate our comrade, WILLIAM McKINLEY, whose record as a soldier, statesman and patriot has won for him the respect and admiration of the civilized world, on the prospect of his being called to the highest executive office of the country he fought to preserve; and

Resolved further, That we rejoice that this Encampment is honored by containing on its roll of members one whose record and worth have brought to him this deserved recognition and high endorsement from a large and representative body of his fellow countrymen.

Adopted.

THEODORE JONES, *Colonel,*
C. C. HIGGINS, *Adjutant,*
LLOYD MEYERS,
J. ED. MINNICH,
WARNER MILLS,
Committee.

TIPPECANOE VETERANS ALSO.

On the same day Major McKINLEY was also presented with the following address:

The Old Tippecanoe Club of Chicago, Illinois, organized in 1888 by veterans who voted in 1840 for General WILLIAM HENRY HARRISON for President of the United States, congratulates the country upon the nomination by the Republican National Convention of Hon. WILLIAM McKINLEY for that high office. We feel confident of his triumphant election, and believe that under his administration the cardinal principle for which the members of this Club have always contended, American protection to American industries and American labor will be readopted into law and permanently sustained. With reciprocity in trade, and the currency intact at one hundred cents on the dollar, according to the Republican platform, the dignity as well as the financial honor and integrity of the Nation will be inviolably maintained, and the hum of diversified industry, everywhere resounding throughout the land, will be evidence conclusive of returned and enduring prosperity, and of happiness and contentment among all the people.

Unanimously adopted, June 27, 1896.

THOMAS GOODMAN, *President.*
C. R. HAGERTY, *Secretary.*

OLD MEDINA CONGRATULATES BOTH NOMINEES.

Hon. GARRET A. HOBART, of New Jersey, the Republican candidate for Vice President, arrived at Canton, via the Pennsylvania lines, on Tuesday morning, June 30th. He was met at the depot by Major McKINLEY and driven in his carriage to the McKinley home, there being no public demonstrations, in deference to the wishes of both candidates. It happened, however, that soon after the arrival of Mr. HOBART, several hundred of the leading citizens of Medina County, Ohio, arrived via Massillon on the Interurban Electric Railway, and were escorted to Major McKINLEY's residence by the Canton Troop of Invincible Republicans. The visitors came from Medina, Wadsworth, Lodi, River Styx, and other points in Medina County, and were headed by the Lodi Band. The Medina Glee Club, also accompanied them and sang "In A Little While," and other campaign airs effectively. The "Old Guard at Orrville," in 1884, as one of the campaign banners called them, was also numerously represented. Judge ALBERT MUNSON, of Medina, who had the honor of presenting Major McKINLEY's name in both the conventions at Orrville in 1884, and again in 1890, was now selected by his friends to introduce them to "the next President." He said:

"Major McKINLEY: We come to-day upon no political errand, but to renew the old friendships that were made in 1884 and to pledge anew our fealty to the principles of the grand old party which you so ably represent as its Presidential candidate in the pending campaign. The years as they have passed into history since 1884 have made great changes in men, parties and events. But one thing we know, principles never change. They are eternal; they withstand the wreck of time and the decay and dissolution of nations. The record of the Republican party stands without a peer in the history of political organizations. Its fame is secure; neither time, nor the changes made by time, in the wreck of kingdoms and principalities, which is sure to come in the onward flow of events, in nature's unbending order, will ever dim or efface the brilliancy of the record of the grand old party." [Judge Munson then spoke at some length of the Republican party and its record, contrasting it with the unfulfilled promises of the Democratic party, and in conclusion said:] "Should it be your mission, of which we have no doubt, to lead this great people out of the wilderness of distress and unrest up into the highlands of a broad and expanding industrial prosperity, you will be hailed and recognized as a public benefactor in every town, village, and city of the great Republic." (Applause.)

Major McKinley's Response.

"JUDGE MUNSON AND MY FELLOW-CITIZENS: I would not conceal my gratification at this friendly call from my old friends and former constituents of Medina County. I recall that in my public career the people of Medina County rendered devoted and unwavering service to the Republican cause, of which, for the moment, I stood by designation of my party, as its standard-bearer, in two important Congressional contests. Twelve years ago, as is known to most of you, by an act of the State Legislature, your county was placed in my Congressional district. The district was believed to be Democratic, and was made to be Democratic; and I shall never forget that in that contest your grand old county gave for the Republican candidate the largest majority it had ever given in its history, and saved the district to the Republican cause. (Great applause.) I recall, too, that in 1890, the last Congressional race I ever made, in another district believed to be reliably Democratic by more than three thousand majority, when the votes were counted out, that by the help of Medina and the other counties of the district, and by the help of men of all parties, too, the three thousand adverse majority had been reduced to three hundred, in the largest vote ever polled in the four counties comprising the district at any election in all its history. Such friendship, devotion and loyalty can never fade from my memory, and your presence here this morning in such large numbers brings to mind a thousand interesting memories connected with those two campaigns. (Applause.) Medina County has always stood by the Republican cause, because she has believed that enveloped in that cause were the best interests and highest prosperity of the American people. (Applause.) I thank you, my fellow citizens, not only for your devotion to Republican principles in the past, but for your devotion to home and country both in peace and war, at every point in our history. This patriotic zeal I warmly commend, (cheers,) and I thank your venerable Chairman, my good old friend, Judge Munson for his and your assurance of support of the same principles in the future. We have with us this morning, and can consider ourselves most fortunate—the nominee of the great Republican party for Vice President of the United States, GARRET A. HOBART, of New Jersey. (Cries of 'Hurrah for Hobart!') I know you will be delighted to see and hear from him, and it gives me exceptional pleasure to be able to present him to you." (Great applause.)

MR. HOBART'S ADDRESS.

As Mr. HOBART stepped to the edge of the porch there was another demonstration in his honor, and three hearty cheers were given him. The people were evidently delighted with his appearance, and were bound that he should know it. When comparative silence was secured, he said:

"MAJOR MCKINLEY, GENTLEMEN OF MEDINA COUNTY, AND FELLOW CITIZENS OF OHIO: I thank you for the compliment of this call, but I must say at the same time that I am not gifted, as our friend Major McKinley is in the graces of oratory and ease of diction that will permit me to talk long to you. (Cries of 'Go on.') I think I should speak but briefly on this occasion, when my only business is to pay my respects to your most distinguished fellow citizen, Major McKinley. (Applause.) But New Jersey, gentlemen, feels very near to Ohio these days. (Laughter.) In the great Republican convention lately held in St. Louis there were no more constant friends, no more devoted admirers of your Major McKINLEY than were the delegates from the State of New Jersey. (Cheers and applause.) We feel, too, gentlemen, that we have some little right to say a word in a Republican convention nowadays, for last November we carried the State of New Jersey for the Republican party by the grand majority of twenty-seven thousand, nine hundred votes. (Great applause.) New Jersey greets Ohio to-day, and if the Republicans and Democrats both feel then, as it seems they feel now, that we are fighting for National honor or National dishonor, for National prosperity or National bankruptcy, and most of them, as looks rather probable now, vote with us, then New Jersey will greet Ohio next November with a Republican majority of not less than fifty thousand votes. (Applause.) I thank you, gentlemen, for the compliment of your call but I did not intend to try to make a speech. I will be glad, however, to meet as many of you personally as possible during the interval which you spend here to-day." (Great applause.)

Then both Major McKINLEY and Mr. HOBART shook hands with hundreds of the big crowd before it dispersed, evidently very much pleased with their candidates. Mr. HOBART was tendered a reception by the various Republican Clubs of Canton that evening, but was obliged to return East via Cleveland immediately.

PITTSBURG LAWYERS CALL.

The Allegheny County (Pittsburg) Bar Association, embracing a membership of more than three hundred attorneys, had spent the day (June 30th) at Congress Lake, Stark Country, twelve miles north of Canton, having come from Pittsburg that morning by special train over the C., C. & S. Railroad. On their return trip, it was decided by the Association to call and pay their respects to Major McKINLEY, the party to march to his residence, headed by Thayer's Band, and a Committee consisting of Judges WHITE, SLAGLE, OVER and MAGEE, of the Allegheny County Bench, with Judge GEORGE E. BALDWIN, of Canton, as honary escort. Here the company were presented by Judge WHITE in the following address:

Major McKINLEY: The Pittsburg Bar is as fine a lot of men as you ever laid eyes on. (Laughter.) After spending the day in one of the most delightful places in the State of Ohio, or Pennsylvania, or any other State, we thought it would not do to pass through Canton without calling upon you. We do not want you to make any speech, and do not expect you to shak hands with us; you must not do it. We simply want to see you because we have seen some little about you in the newspapers. (Laughter and applause.) We wanted to see the young soldier who left college to join the grand army of the Republic as a private, not going in as a commissioned officer. We wanted to see the boy who served during the war and by his faithfulness as a private soldier got to an honorable position in the Army upon a promotion given him by ABRAHAM LINCOLN for 'gallant and meritorious conduct in battle.' (Applause.) Then we wanted to see what ROBERT BURNS says is the 'noblest work of God—an honest man.' (Loud cheering.) We wanted to see a pure representative of the human family, a good citizen—the highest honor or title that can be conferred upon any one—a good American citizen." (Applause.)

34

Major McKinley's Response.

"JUDGE WHITE AND MEMBERS OF THE BENCH AND BAR OF ALLEGHENY COUNTY: I have no purpose to inflict a speech upon you, but I can not refrain presenting myself long enough to thank you for the compliment and honor of this call, for I deem it both a high compliment and distinguished honor to have the gentlemen of the legal profession of the great, busy, pushing, progressive city of Pittsburg call upon me at my home. (Applause.) I regretted that my engagements would not permit my joining you in the pleasures at Congress Lake to-day—and it was only engagements already made, which could not be set aside, that prevented my being with you in person, as I was with you in thought and good will. (Cheers.) I thank your spokesman for his touching, generous and eloquent words, and if it had not been prohibited, I would have been very glad to shake each of you by the hand. (Laughter.) But as it has been, I must not disregard the order of the court, although I believe you are now beyond Judge WHITE's jurisdiction." (Laughter and applause.)

Three hearty cheers "for the next President" were then given, and then three cheers and a tiger again, and then there was a general rush to greet Major McKINLEY. No one could respect the injunction of even Judge WHITE when it came to that.

VISITORS FROM ST. LOUIS.

Hon. RICHARD C. KERENS and party, of St. Louis, arrived at Canton via the Pan Handle and C., C. and S. Railroads, Wednesday afternoon, July 1st. The visitors were representative business men and Republicans in Missouri, and included C. H. SPENCER, S. A. BEMIS, ex-Governor E. O. STANNARD, Mayor HASTINGS, of Sedalia, and C. G. WARNER. They were received by Major McKINLEY in his library, where a short address was read by Mr. KERENS, as follows:

"Major McKINLEY: We come to tender you our fervent congratulations both on your nomination and the excellent outlook for your election and Republican success generally. We endorse and espouse every word of the Republican Party's platform, and refer with shame to the abrogation of the reciprocity treaties whereby, in one instance alone, there was taken from the great valley of the Mississippi a flourishing and remunerative trade with the West Indies in breadstuffs, which amounted to millions annually, and which was ruthlessly stricken down without reason or pretense of benefit to anybody. We do not disparage the money question; the Republican party has always been sound in its financial policies. But we do insist that the policy of protection to American industries, affecting us it does the wage-earner, the manufacturer, the producer of every class, is of paramount importance; that the goods and wares consumed by our people shall be manufactured in our country, furnishing employment to millions and stopping the flow of gold which under free trade conditions goes to the other world—goes to pay for manufactured articles freely admitted to our excellent home market in competition with our formerly prosperous and independent laborers, although made by the poorly paid wage-earners of foreign countries. The Republican party, on its record, can be trusted to furnish the best money of the civilized world; the Democratic party just the reverse, and we hold its free trade policy directly responsible for nine-tenths of the depression, the reduction in wages, the armies of unemployed, the depreciation in values the country over. In one instance alone, that of railway securities, the depreciation in values has amounted to thousands of millions of dollars."

Major McKinley's Response.

"GENTLEMEN: I appreciate highly the call of this representative body of business men of the city of St. Louis and the State of Missouri, and thank you for your expressions of regard and good will. I feel that in the address that has been read to me, you have made a strong argument. What we want is a restoration of the American economic policy which lasted for more than thirty years, and under which we enjoyed exceptional prosperity. What the Republican party has done in the past for the country, it can be relied upon to do in the future. It should be a matter of pride and gratification to us all that the party, although only a little more than a third of a century old, has never failed to meet every demand and exigency of the Government, however gloomy the outlook, or desperate the condition of the country, when it was called to power. History repeats itself, and I am sure that if the cardinal doctrines of the Republican party, Protection, Reciprocity and Sound Money, can be carried by a pronounced majority this year, confidence will again be quickly restored. After all, confidence has everything to do with the business of the country, and when was it ever more badly needed than now, and to what source can it be looked for if not to the Republican party? This the people fully realize, and by their votes will decree that we shall enter upon an era of better times, which, I believe, will last for many years."

THE CHRISTIAN ENDEAVORERS.

The annual State Convention of the Christian Endeavor Society of Ohio was in session in Canton for a fortnight preceding Wednesday, July 1st. On that afternoon about five thousand of its members, women and men, repaired to Major McKINLEY'S residence and were introduced by Mr. J. H. BOMBERGER, of Mansfield, President of the State Society. In reply to his address Major McKINLEY spoke to the great host as follows:

"MR. BOMBERGER AND LADIES AND GENTLEMEN OF THE CHRISTIAN ENDEAVOR SOCIETY OF THE STATE OF OHIO: It gives me sincere pleasure to welcome you, and your Society in this delegated capacity, to my home, and I thank you, all for the courtesy and warmth of your greeting. The people of Canton are glad to have you among them and in their behalf, as well as my own, I feel free to bid you a hearty and hospitable welcome. (Cheers.) Free governments have uniformly recognized their dependence upon a Higher Power and taken steps to promote morality and the diffusion of knowledge among their citizens. In the United States this has been steadily the aim of our local and State governments, and in the advancement of this great work all good people, without respect to the denominational connections, have had an active and useful part. In every proper, charitable, broad and generous effort, I bid you godspeed, and commend to your observance, and for your example, that lofty and noble policy, that truly patriotic and philanthropic devotion to the amelioration and uplifting of mankind, which so conspicuously distinguished the founders of this mighty, free Republic. Let us cherish the institutions of civil and

-eligious liberty which they planted in the wilderness, and that have been so signally preserved for us to the present hour, and continue them in all their vigor, strength and beauty for countless generations yet to come. A higher respect for these institutions, a deeper reverence of law, a closer attention to the requirements of good citizenship, a wider inculcation of the spirit of charity, forbearance and good will to all, and a more constant and earnest endeavor for the enlightenment and advancement of all our people, can not, I am sure, but be in keeping with the purposes of Almighty God toward this greatly favored Nation, and to you who may engage in this noble work, and to all who are so engaged everywhere, I devoutly wish the fullest measure of success and happiness." (Great applause.)

The grand old National anthem "*America*" was sung by the people and then came the rush to shake hands, and for nearly an hour Major McKinley was busy receiving the happy throng. It was a most enthusiastic meeting.

THOUSANDS OF TUSCARAWAS PROTECTIONISTS.

Thousands of Tuscarawas County men came to Canton, Friday, July 3rd, to pay their respects to the man of their choice for President. They came over a special train on the C., L. E. and W. Railroad to Justus, where a transfer was made to the C., C. and S. Railroad, on which they came to Canton, after trips of from twenty-five to forty miles. The delegation was headed by the Great Eastern Band, of New Philadelphia, and the Boys Drum Corps, of Canal Dover. The Tuscarawas delegation was composed largely of employes of the iron and tin mills in Dennison, Uhrichsville, New Philadelphia and Canal Dover. They carried several unique banners. Near the head of the column was a great banner made of tin, said to be the largest sheet of bright tin ever made in any country. It was thirty gauge thirty inches wide and twelve feet long. It was the product of the American Tin Plate Machine and Manufacturing Company and the Reeves Iron Company, the latter company rolling the black plate and the former coating it with tin. On one side of the banner, which was borne at the head of a long staff, was the inscription: "Largest sheet ever made," and on the reverse side the words: "Give us McKinley and Protection and we will make it larger." A score of men carried a strip of jointed tin sixty feet long bearing the name of the candidates: "Our choice, McKINLEY AND HOBART!" Six employes of the New Philadelphia Iron and Steel Company carried a plate of galvanized iron which was said to be the largest sheet of that kind ever rolled. It was thirty inches wide and two hundred and fifty-five inches long. On the top of the decorated frame which supported it was a portrait of Major McKinley—and all these interesting souvenirs were presented to him before the delegation departed. Arriving at the McKinley residence, the band and drum corps each gave a selection, and then Col W. A. Bovey, of Dennison, stepped forward and addressed Major McKinley, who had come upon the veranda, as follows:

"Major McKINLEY: We have come to your beautiful city and home this afternoon not as a crowd of curiosity seekers, but we are here as friends and neighbors in the strictest and most truthful acceptation of those terms. There is no class of labor or occupation but what is represented in this delegation. (Cheers.) In you we behold the typical American. In you, sir, these laborers and mechanics recognize one who has stood before the people at all times—in victory and defeat—and proclaimed protection to American industry.

37

(Cheers.) Your loyalty, sir, to 'Old Glory,' too, is dear to the heart of every lover of this country, and is so esteemed that it will never be forgotten until 'life's fitful dream is o'er.' We are here to pledge ourselves from this time forward to every effort to place you in the Presidential chair, and we know from your past history that it will be honored for your sitting there." (Applause and loud cheers for "McKinley!")

Major McKinley's Response.

In reply to their friendly greeting, Major McKinley stepped upon a chair at his door step and spoke to his visitors, as follows:

"Colonel Bovey and My Fellow Citizens: I am very grateful for this visit on the part of my friends in Tuscarawas County, and I thank my old friend, your spokesman, for the cordial, generous and eloquent words of greeting which he has tendered in your behalf. This assemblage is fairly typical of our American communities, and fitly represents the varied occupations of the American people. As your spokesman has well said, in this audience are farmers, laborers, mechanics, miners, railroad employes, professional men—representatives of every rank and class of people. You are here, too, far from your homes, not from curiosity nor considerations at all personal, but because in your hearts you believe in the great fundamental doctrines of the Republican party. (Loud applause.) You believe that those principles are best for you whenever and wherever put into practical legislation and administration. You believe that those principles will secure to our people the largest measure of good to the greatest number, and you believe that, too, because you recall that for more than a third of a century these great Republican principles dominated legislation and administration in this country, and that during all that period you enjoyed exceptional prosperity, something you have not known the last three years and a half. (Loud applause.) You know, therefore, something of these great principles from experience, which, after all, is the most unerring teacher, and you are eagerly waiting for the opportunity to express the lessons of that experience in your votes next November. (Cheers and cries of 'That's right,' and 'Wish the election was tomorrow.') All these demonstrations that have been witnessed here for the past two weeks are only significant because they show what is in the hearts of the American people, that they want an opportunity—and they want it soon, too—to return to power that grand old party, to which your spokesman has so feelingly alluded, in every branch of the Government of the United States. Here in this country we are dependent upon each other, no matter what our occupation may be. All of us want good times, good wages, good prices, good markets, and then we want good money, too, and always intend to have it. (Vociferous cheering.) When we give a good day's work to our employers we want to be paid in good sound dollars, worth one hundred cents each, and never any less. Now, whatever policy will bring back these good times is the one that the great majority of the American people favor, and will register their votes for at the coming election—and you seem to have made up your minds just what that policy is. (Applause.) What I want to see in this country is a return to that prosperity which we enjoyed for thirty years—prior to 1893. (Loud and continuous applause.) A policy that will put idle men at work at American wages (loud applause,) for the more men wo have at work at good American wages the better markets the farmers will have and the better prices they will get for their products.

Every farmer here knows that from experience. (Applause.) And now it will give me great pleasure to meet and greet all of you." (Tremendous applause and cheers.)

COLORED CALLERS FROM STARK COUNTY.

It was nearly ten o'clock Friday night, July 3rd, when delegations of colored people came from Canton, Massillon, Alliance, and other points in Stark County to call on Major McKinley. There were several hundred visitors, with glee clubs, a drum corps, mandolin quartet and other musical features. WILLIAM BELL, of Massillon, acted as spokesman for them, and greeted Major McKinley with a few well chosen sentences expressive of the regard of the colored people for him. "You have always treated us, just as you do everybody else," said Mr. BELL, "with great consideration and kindness, and on every occasion have been our friend, champion and protector. We come to congratulate you and assure you of our earnest support until you are triumphantly elected next November." (Great applause.)

Major McKinley's Response.

"Mr. BELL AND MY FELLOW CITIZENS OF STARK COUNTY: I am glad to meet you and receive your greetings and congratulations. But the congratulations should be on the other side, for I feel like congratulating all of you upon the splendid progress which your race has made since emancipation. There is no name, I take it, so near and dear to you as that of the martyred President ABRAHAM LINCOLN, the emancipator of your race, and while he has long since gone to his reward, and is out of human sight he will live in human memory, not simply in the memories of your people, but of all mankind everywhere forever more. He was the most splendid type of the true and heroic American. He loved all the races of men, and no one ever felt abashed in his presence. One of the most impressive monuments to be found in Washington, the Capital City of our country, is a bronze statue to Mr. LINCOLN, erected by the men and women of your race. It is on the East Side of the great Capitol Building in what is known as Lincoln Park. It was conceived, erected and paid for by people who had been made free by the immortal Proclamation, and it should be a matter of pride to you, when you know that the first contribution received towards th. .rection of that bronze statue was from a colored women of the State of Ohio, living in the city of Marietta, who gave the first money she earned as a free woman to the erection of this splendid monum .t. (Cheers.) It was a proper tribute to Mr. LINCOLN's great work and p nory. He was ever mindful of your race. Long before you were given .· elective franchise, Mr. LINCOLN wrote to MICHAEL HAHN, the First Free .ate Governor of Louisiana, that he thought the right to vote should be given to the colored men, and 'especially the very intelligent and those who fought gallantly in our ranks,' and then he closed with these beautiful words: 'They would probably help, in some trying time to come, to keep the jewel of liberty within the family of freedom.' (Cries of 'Good' and applause.) I thank you, fellow citizens, for this kind, friendly call. I know that you love the cause and the party with which Mr. LINCOLN's name will be forever associated. I know you love the great

39

cardinal principles of the Republican party. (A voice, 'You bet your life') and I am very sure you will be found at all times standing for the best things in government—that which will secure the greatest good to the greatest number." (Applause.)

A reception was then held, after which three hearty cheers were given for Major McKinley, and a strong and characteristic address was made by Judge George E. Baldwin, of Canton. Following Judge Baldwin, Hon. Robert A. Pinn, the eloquent colored lawyer of Massilon, delivered a short address.

A BUGLE CALL TO THE NATION.

The call made upon Major McKinley by the Thirty-Second Ward Foraker Club, of Cleveland, on Saturday, July 11th, was a signal success, and the Forest City visitors enjoyed it immensely. They came at 4:15 o'clock via the C., C. and S. Railroad, and headed by Kirk's Military Band and the Canton Troop, proceeded immediately to the McKinley residence. At the house the band played the "Star Spangled Banner," and Major McKinley's appearance was the signal for a hearty cheer. As he stepped to the front o' the porch, D. H. Lucas, President of the Club, delivered a spirited address to him, which was frequently applauded. He said:

"Major McKinley and Friends: The members of the Thirty-Second Ward Foraker Club, of Cleveland, have assumed the privilege of coming to Canton to show our appreciation of the result at St. Louis, and to extend our sincere congratulations. We stand firmly by the Republican party and its principles. We have been with you at the State Convention and in the National Convention, we have always loved to follow you, and will put our armor on and stand more strongly by you during this campaign than ever." (Applause.)

Major McKinley's Response.

When Mr. Lucas concluded, Major McKinley stepped upon a chair to respond. He was greeted with a storm of applause and as the address proceeded each point was loudly cheered from beginning to end. He said:
"Mr. President, Ladies and Gentlemen: It gives me great pleasure to welcome you to this city and to my home, for I highly appreciate the honor and compliment of this call. I thank you for your congratulations, and the assurances of support you offer for the great principles for which the Republican party stands this year. (Applause.) I congratulate you, in turn, upon having chosen for your name the name of one of the most distinguished leaders of our party and country, Joseph B. Foraker, of Ohio. (Applause.) Recent events have imposed upon patriotic people a responsibility and duty greater than any they have known since the Civil War. Then it was a struggle to preserve the Government of the United States; now it is a struggle to preserve the financial honor of the Government of the United States. (Cries of 'Yes,' and applause.) Then it was a contest to save the Union; now it is a contest to save spotless its credit. (Great applause.) Then section was arrayed against section; now men of all sections can unite, and will unite, to rebuke the repudiation of our obligations and the debasement of our currency. (Applause.) In this contest patriotism is above party, and National honor dearer than any party name. The currency and credit of the Government are

40

good now and must be kept good forever. Our trouble is not with the character of the money that we have, but with the threat to debase it. We have the same currency that we had in 1892—good the world over and unquestioned by any people. Then, too, we had unexampled credit and prosperity. Our difficulty now is to get that money into circulation and invested in productive enterprises which furnish employment to American labor. (Great applause.) This is impossible with the distrust that hangs over the country at the present time, and every effort to make our dollars, or any one of them worth less than one hundred cents each only serves to increase that distrust. What we want is a sound policy, financial and industrial, which will give courage and confidence to all, for when that is secured the money now unemployed because of fear for the future, and lack of confidence in investment, will quickly appear in the channel of trade. (Cries of 'You're right, Major,' and applause.) The employment of our idle money, the idle money that we already have, in gainful pursuits, will put every idle man in the country at work, and when there is work there is wages, and when there is work and wages there are consumers at home, who constitute the best market for the products of our soil. (Great applause.) Having destroyed business and confidence by a free trade policy, it is now proposed to make things still worse by entering upon an era of depreciated currency. Not content with the inauguration of the ruinous policy which has brought down the wages of the laborer and the price of farm products, its advocates now offer a new policy which will diminish the value of the money in which wages and products are paid. (Applause.) Against both policies we stand opposed. Our creed embraces an honest dollar, an untarnished National credit, adequate revenues for the use of the Government, protection to labor and enterprise, preservation of the home market, and a reciprocity that will extend our foreign markets. Upon this platform we stand and submit its declarations to the sober and considerate judgment of the American people. (Great applause.) I thank you again, my fellow citizens, for this call and greeting, and it will give me very great pleasure, ladies and gentlemen, to meet you all personally." (Applause.)

LINCOLN SENDS GREETING.

Major McKinley received on Tuesday morning, July 14th, the following cheering message from one of the strongest Republican organizations in the State of Nebraska. His mail, too, contained many similar greetings from prominent men in all sections of the State:

LINCOLN, Nebraska, July 13, 1896.

"I am instructed to send you the following message: The Young Men's Republican Club, stronger in membership and influence than ever before during its nine years existence, in meeting assembled, again sends greeting to WILLIAM McKINLEY, of Ohio, and assure him that in the coming contest the fact that our fellow townsman, WILLIAM J. BRYAN, is the Democratic nominee, will only make our organization more enthusiastic and determined than ever in behalf of the Republican party and its candidates. This county will cast an immense majority for Major McKINLEY. We have been in battle array in this State against Populism until fighting vagaries, such as the Chicago platform, has become the accustomed thing. Situated as we are in the disputed territory, we welcome the conflict and are firm in our conviction that victory will not come to Mr. BRYAN in either this Nation, State, or County.

[Signed]   JOHN B. CUNNINGHAM *President*

41

THE WOMEN OF CLEVELAND AND NORTHERN OHIO.

Rain interfered with, but did not set aside the plans of the women of Cleveland and Northern Ohio, who had determined to visit Canton and extend their congratulations and best wishes to Major McKinley. Their special train pulled into the C., C. and S. depot shortly after noon, Wednesday, July 15th, a little behind time, but the six hundred people which filled the eight coaches found awaiting them a detachment of the Canton Troop, a committee of the Canton Sorosis, and a large number of other Canton people. In a short time a parade was organized and on the way to the McKinley home. The horsemen led and the Woman's Band, of Chagrin Falls, Ohio, followed. The populace of the city turned out *en masse* to witness the unique parade, and it was a matter of general comment that the gay and varied costumes of the ladies produced a much finer effect than had the best efforts of the men, with all their campaign regalia. When the McKinley home was reached, except as to the personnel of the crowd, there was little distinction between this visit and that of the scores of other delegations who have come to Canton to greet the Republican nominee for President. The spokesman of this delegation enjoys a distinction shared by few other women in Ohio. She is a member of the Cleveland Board of Education, and was regularly elected as the nominee of the Republican party—Mrs. Elroy M. Avery, whose husband is prominent as a Republican member of the Ohio Senate. Her address, which was most enthusiastically received, was as follows:

"Major McKinley: We come from Cleveland, Cleveland, the beautiful. Cleveland that still lives, the Queen City of the Lower Lakes, the great heart of the Western Reserve, that gave Giddings, Wade and Garfield to the Nation; a city of great American industries that are suffering from un-American legislation; an unfortified city on the border, facing the Canadian shore, but recognizing that our best protection against foreign aggression is a protective tariff. Coming from a city of a hundred years to-day, we turn aside from our Centennial to do homage to the man who best represents the great American idea, under the fostering care of which we hope Cleveland will gloriously flourish and bravely celebrate her second hundredth year. We come to greet you, not as politicians, but as women, wives, mothers and sisters. We can not cast one vote for you, and yet we love our country,

"'The mighty mother of a mighty brood.'

Our country, that 'lifts up the manhood' of the nations of the earth—and we desire and through you we seek, her prosperity and glory. We believe in the highest destiny for this American nation to which we belong; we may not fully appreciate man-made political platforms; but we better understand the significance of current events than some folks give us credit for; we know that when you enter at the door of the White House, peace and comfort will enter at our doors; that when you receive your heritage by the decree of a grateful people, our husbands and fathers will receive the fruits of their industry, and the heart of the wife and mother will be made glad. When the husband lacks work, the wife knows and feels it, though she will still cheer and comfort; when the factory fires are out, the fire in the hearth burns low; when the spindles cease to turn, poverty and hunger stalk through the streets by day; when the anvil no longer rings, misery and wailing brood in the home by night. Who shall say that woman has no interest in your success? Every woman has a living interest in the money question. If our husbands earn the money, we spend and intend to spend it. Without pleading guilty to the charge of a weakness for the bargain counter, every thrifty woman wants her few dollars to have as great a purchasing power as possible, to be worth a hundred cents, not fifty, to be convertible into twenty pounds of sugar, not ten. We stand ready to welcome every one who refuses to dwell longer in the tents of the opposition, and to bind up the wounds of every one, who breaking loose from the already disintegrating ranks of the opposition, and placing patriotism above party, pledges his support to the "Advance Agent of Prosperity." Each recruit will find the silver lining of his cloud fringed with the higher glory of the morning's golden glow and be lulled to peaceful rest by the melodious chant of our political household. Descended from Revolutionary stock, and from those who were

'Prompt to assert by manners, voice and pen,
Or ruder arms, their rights as Englishmen,'

you stand before the Nation and the world, as a typical American,

'With the stern high-featured beauty
Of plain devotedness to duty.'

He who represents our Nation to the world should be an unblemished gentleman. As a soldier, brave and faithful in days of war, we bring you our garlands of honor; as a statesman, wise and just, we bring you our cordial greeting; as a son and husband, we bring you our grateful homage. Among men your name stands as a synonym for protection to American industry; it stands for sound money and reciprocity, and freedom, too, from ocean to ocean. Among women it stands for more than that. It stands for protection for the home. it stands for right-thinking and right living; it stands for tenderness to mother and for love to wife, for all that makes the American home the dearest spot on earth, the footprint of God. In honoring your mother and your wife you have honored womankind. You are very dear to Ohio, but Ohio gives you to the Nation; henceforth you belong to the whole people. Through you, as we devoutly hope and fervently pray, the Almighty will work out for us a glorious destiny, clothing our sons and daughters with prosperity and honor, and making America the beacon star for all the nations of the earth. The prayers and blessings of the women of the Western Reserve go with you as you go forth on that high mission." (Great applause.)

Major McKinley's Response.

Major McKinley was greeted by the waving of handkerchiefs and cheers from hundreds of feminine voices. He spoke as follows:

"Mrs. Avery and Women of Cleveland and Northern Ohio: I greatly appreciate this friendly call, and assure you that I do not undervalue the gracious message of congratulation and confidence which you have so eloquently delivered. It is an assurance of the deep interest which you feel, and which should be felt by every family in the land, in the public questions of the day and their rightful settlement at the polls. There is no limitation to the influence that may be exerted by woman in the United States, and no adequate tribute can be paid to her service to mankind throughout its eventful history. At the distance period of its settlement, in the days of the Revolution, in the trials of Western pioneer life, during the more recent but dread days of our Civil War—indeed, at every step of our progress as a Nation, the devotion

43

and sacrifices of women were constantly apparent and often conspicuous. (Applause.) She was everywhere appreciated and recognized, though God alone could place her service at its true value. The work of woman has been a power in every emergency and always for good. In calamity and distress she has ever been helpful and heroic; not only have some of the brightest pages of our National history been illumined by her splendid example and noble efforts for the public good, but her influence in the home, the church, the school and the community in moulding character for every profession and duty to which our race is called has been potential and sublime. But it is in the peaceful walks of life where her power is greatest and most beneficial. One of the tenderest passages to me in the works of JOHN STUART MILL beautifully expresses this thought. It is recorded in his Autobiography, when he paused to pay high and deserved tribute to his wife, of whom he could not say too much. He says: 'She was not only the author of many of the best things I did, but she inspired every good thing I did.' Many men there are from whom frankness would not withhold, but would command, like expression of obligation to woman, wife, mother, sister, or friend. (Great applause.) One of the best things of our civilization in America is the constant advancement of woman to a higher plane of labor and responsibility. The opportunities for her are greater now than ever before. This is singularly true here in the United States, where practically every avenue of human endeavor is open to her. Her impress is felt in art, science, literature, song, and government. Our churches, our schools, our charities, our professions, and our general business interests are more than ever each year directed by her. Respect for womankind has become with us a National characteristic; and what a high, noble, manly trait it is—none nobler, or holier! It stamps the true gentleman; the man who loves wife, mother and home will respect and reverence all womankind, and he is always the better citizen for such gentle breeding. The home over which the trusted wife presides is the citadel of our strength, the best guarantee of good citizenship and sound morals in government. It is at the foundation—upon it all else is constructed. From the plain American home 'where virtue dwells and truth hath her abiding place,' go forth the men and women who make the great States and cities which adorn our Republic, which maintain law and order—that citizenship which aims only at the public welfare, the common good of all. Some one has said that

'Women mould the future as mothers,
And govern the present as wives.'

I congratulate you upon what woman has done for grand and noble objects in the past, and I rejoice with you at the wider and broader field of the present, and the splendid vista of the future everywhere opening for you. I again thank you for your presence here and for this manifestation of regard and good will. Mrs. McKINLEY and I will be happy to meet and greet you all." (Great applause.)

The hymn composed for the occasion by Mrs. N. COE STEWART, was then sung; Mrs. MARY ELLSWORTH CLARK, of Cleveland, as solo, in a rich voice leading the chorus, and the Woman's Band playing the accompaniment. The words of the hymn are as follows:

A PRAYER FOR THE NATION.

Ring out bells of freedom, ring long and ring loud,
The sunshine is piercing the dark, threat'ning cloud;
'Tis bright'ning the stars on Old Glory unfurled,
Which speaks like a god to a wondering world.

44

The brave toiling millions who bend to the yoke,
Whose sweat drops are prayers, though a word be not spoke,
Are swelling the chorus which sweeps to the sea—
McKinley, McKinley, our Captain shall be."

CHORUS:
God keep him, the true and the brave,
Our beautiful country to save;
Bends low a great Nation to crave
This boon at Thy hand.

"McKinley, McKinley," the children all shout,
The star-begemmed banner he fought for fling out:
The home shall be sacred, its walls firmly stand,
When honor and manhood rule proudly the land.

McKinley, McKinley, the world waits for thee,
Humanity pleads with the land of the free,
That God in great mercy will keep thee to stand,
A rock of defense in our glorious land.

Flowers for Mrs. McKinley.

Miss BIRDELLE SWITZER, Society Editor of the Cleveland Plain Dealer, then stepped forward, and handed Mrs. McKINLEY a large basket of roses, a present from the young ladies in the party. In presenting the flowers, she said:

"Mrs. McKINLEY: I bring you in behalf of the young women of Cleveland a basket of roses. These American Beauties represent the queen of flowers, as you, by your sweet womanliness and grace, have won the right to represent the American queen of the home. These white blossoms are a symbol of that pure spirit we have learned to reverence, and this blue, the truth that is mirrored in your eyes, has caused the heart of your husband to trust in you. We can not all hope to win Presidents for husbands, but your example as a wife is before us, and following that, we can at least aid our future companions to be worthy men. If each beautiful thought your countrywomen have in mind for you were a rose, the streets of Canton would be filled to overflowing with a fragrant tribute, whose odor would forever linger in your memory. Allow me,

'Sweets to the sweet."

Mrs. McKINLEY acknowledged the gift with a smile and a bow. Major McKINLEY was also given a box of artificial flowers sent him by Miss TERESSA DOTTERWICK, of Cleveland, who has been confined to her bed for six years, but desired to make something for the next President. An informal reception concluded the exercises. Major McKINLEY shook hands with the ladies, and after a few words with Mrs. McKINLEY, they passed happily along to the Tabernacle where a lunch was served in their honor by the hospitable people of Canton.

COMRADES FROM CLEVELAND.

The visit of the Cuyahoga Country Soldiers and Sailors Union to Major McKINLEY on Thursday afternoon, July 16th, was one of the most notable and impressive calls he has received since his nomination for President. The Cleveland, Terminal and Valley train bringing the party to Canton arrived about 3:30 o'clock. Canton Troop was in waiting as were also two hundred Canton veterans from George D. Harter and Canton Posts. The local G. A. R. acted as escorts and preceded by the horsemen led the procession. The

Cleveland delegation, headed by Fay's Military Band, numbering about three hundred, was in charge of Commander Hugh Buckley, Jr., with J. C. Shields, Captain of the famous Nineteenth Ohio Battery, Marshal of the parade. When Major McKinley appeared upon the porch, cheer after cheer greeted him, and it was several minutes before order was restored. Commander Buckley then said: "Major McKinley: We have come here to tender to you the right hand of comradeship, and to congratulate you upon your nomination as the standard bearer of the Republican party." (Applause.) He then introduced Hon. William T. Clark, State Senator from Cleveland, who presided at the meeting and introduced the other speakers, and who spoke as follows:

"Major McKinley: Your comrades of Cuyahoga County greet you as a comrade during the four years of civil strife from 1861 to 1865. The sweetest words to a comrade are the expressions of friendship and appreciation from those with whom he fought for the maintenance of the flag. Now let us give three cheers again for Major McKinley"—and they were given with a will.

Rev. George W. Pepper, ex-Consul to Milan, was then introduced and spoke as follows: "Major McKinley: There was a time in Athens when there was profound silence, and strangers visiting the city asked the reason, and they were told that Demosthenes was speaking in the assembly of the people. So at this hour there is but one name spoken with admiration throughout this great Nation. It is the magic name of the soldier, the patriot, the Christian gentleman, William McKinley. It is not only mentioned with affection here in his beloved home, but everywhere throughout the Republic, from the valley of the Sacramento, in the golden gorges of the Uba, in the cities and hamlets of the South, by our lakes and rivers, upon the summits of our tallest mountains, and in the depth of our deepest valleys—wherever there is an American heart it thrills at the remembrance of your intrepid and splendid services to rescue from the grasp of foreign competition the productive industries of the United States, and to secure for millions heaven's greatest gift to man, liberty divine. As your fellow soldiers we come to pay our tribute of love and admiration. We honor you because in the dark and dreary hours of the rebellion your musket as well as your voice was on the side of union and liberty. We honor you, that throughout that tremendous contest when our majestic banner wavered in the breeze you never faltered. We honor you for your devotion; for the courage with which you met the hosts of rebellion and braved the vengeance of your country's enemies. We salute you, illustrious sir, and hail you as the first citizen of the Republic. We love you because the unparalleled and matchless Blaine bequeathed to you his mantle. We tender you thanks and cheers not only for your soldiery courage, but also for your valiant defense of American interests. Your coming triumph rings like blessed music —the silver bell of freedom and prosperity will once more peal through the Nation, another pillar and crown of gold will be added to your escutcheon. I have said that your name is known and honored everywhere. I have heard it abroad where a cloudless sky bends over the faded splendors of Italy. When the tremendous majority of your last election was cabled over the ocean the Italian servant rushed up to the office of the Consul and said: "I know who is to be the next Consul when you leave. "Who is it?" I asked. "His name is William McKinley." She only meant, however, that he was to be the next President and I was to be returned by him. (Laughter.) My remarks would be incomplete if I did not refer to the presence of these noble ladies, whose enthusiastic devotion to their illustrious townsman warrants me to close with this toast: May the United States rise up clothed in radiant health and sacred power, and solemnize, with prosperity, Plenty and Eternal Union; and may these ladies, whose health I now propose, live to be bridesmaids at that festival of love and fortune when our comrade WILLIAM MCKINLEY in inaugurated President of the United States." (Hearty applause.)

Captain E. L. PATTERSON was the third speaker, and said:

"Major MCKINLEY, COMRADES OF CUYAHOGA AND STARK COUNTIES: The men who fought to sustain the Union have great affection for each other. There are no stronger ties to bind men together. We know that the best interests of America will be taken care of, and the industries whereby we get our bread will not be lost sight of, under an administration with WILLIAM MCKINLEY at its head. For the sake of America, we pray that we may again greet you on a more splendid occasion on March 4th next." (Cheers.)

Comrade C. C. DEWSTOE was introduced and said:

"'Major MCKINLEY: The Chairman has introduced me and in doing so he referred to the times when we all stood side by side to preserve the Union saying that we are growing gray and a little stiff through the passing years. We may be getting gray, but we are able to lick Bryanism this year, just the same. (Laughter.) We have come here to pay our tribute to a true American citizen. You have, sir, the respect and esteem of your comrades, we honor you as our highest ideal of citizenship, in time of war and in time of peace. We recognize in you a champion of a mighty cause, the protection and welfare of our homes. You have the love, respect, admiration and approval of your old comrades." (Cheers.)

Captain BOHM, of the Seventh O. V. I., on being introduced, said:

"Major MCKINLEY. This is a day which I have looked forward to with pleasure for three years. I am not a prophet, nor the son of a porphet, but watching the political situation, I have believed that our old comrade under the flag would be chosen to lead the hosts of Republicanism to victory this year. The motto *veni, vidi, vici*, is sure to apply to the Republican party this campaign. Comrades of Cleveland and Canton, let us pray with all the strength of our hearts that the comrade who went with us through the war may lead us to prosperity. May a kind Providence watch and guide him in the future as in the past. May he be the man of the people, for the people and loved by the people for all time." (Great applause.)

Major WILLIAM J. GLEASON, of Cleveland, formerly a prominent Democrat, and a gallant veteran, closed the remarks in an apt address, as follows:

"Major MCKINLEY: It was my fate to be born on foreign soil, but nevertheless America is my home and the country I love. Loving America I love protection for America, and above all the champion of protection, Major WILLIAM MCKINLEY. In our city we have a society against smoke. But if the policy of the party in power continues I don't believe there will be much trouble from smoke. (Laughter.) The party of retrogression proposes to give us a young man with a fifty cent dollar to get us out of trouble, but we want neither. We are not here as politicians to-day, but as American citizens. We hope and pray that Major MCKINLEY, the grand American citizen and able statesman, will be the next President of the United States." (Applause.)

47

Major McKinley's Response.

As Major McKinley stepped upon a chair, the old boys in blue went wild with enthusiasm, cheering as only soldiers know how to cheer for several minutes. After silence was secured, Major McKinley spoke as follows:

"My Comrades and Fellow Citizens: I respond to your call with special gratification; nothing gives me greater pleasure than to meet at my home my comrades of the Civil War. The ties of fraternity and friendship grow stronger and dearer as the years recede, and the Old Guard one by one, is called home. Your presence revives many patriotic memories; it recalls many stiring and glorious events. How vividly they rise before us, and what an inspiration for the right they always are! To have been a faithful soldier of the Union is no less a source of joy in your advancing years and infirmities, than a precious legacy for family and friends. It blesses him who gives and enriches him who receives. It is a record of patriotism and service in the severest trials of our history. (Applause.) We all know something of what that war meant and what it cost; what sacrifice it enacted and for what a holy cause the sacrifice was freely given. Treasure illimitable, suffering indiscribable, and death beyond previous record or comparison. By far the larger number of our old comrades of the Grand Army are sleeping 'in their silent tents' beyond the River. But although death has decimated our ranks it is a consoling reflection that more than a million of our comrades still survive. It is a gratifying thought, too, that those who served their country so faithfully in war have always been among our best and truest citizens in peace. It is the living present, however, and its duties and responsibilities, in which every old soldier is now as always most interested. (Applause.) Each new engagement of the war brought its own peculiar trials and perils to face and bravely overcome. The devotion to discipline and duty which distinguished them then has kept the old soldiers true and steady ever since. (Applause.) They have not faltered and will not falter now. There has been no time since they laid down their arms when we had greater need for patriotic men than now, and the response to the crisis of the hour will come from all sections of our common country. (Great applause.) We have reached a point in our history when all men who love their country must unite to defeat by their ballots the forces which now assault the Nation's honor. The war has been over thirty-one years and as a result we have a reunited country, a Union stronger and freer, a civilization higher and nobler, a freedom broader and more enduring, and a flag more glorious and sacred than ever before, and all of them safe from any enemy, at home or abroad, because the men who a third of a century ago fought in deadly conflict unite now in their masterful might to oppose any enemy who would assail either freedom, Union, or flag. (Cheers.) The struggle which is now upon us involving National good faith and honor will enlist their united and earnest service until those who are arrayed against the fair fame and name of the Republic shall be routed and dispersed. Its glories are the common heritage of us all. What was won in the great conflict belongs just as sacredly to those who lost as to those who triumphed. You meet to-day not as soldiers, but as citizens, interested now in maintaining the credit of the country you served so well, and in restoring prosperity and better times to our goodly heritage. The future is the sacred trust of all, South as well as North. Honesty, like patriotism, can neither be bounded by State nor sectional lines. (Great applause.) Financial dishonor is the threatened danger now, and good men will obliterate old lines of party in a united effort to uphold American credit and honor. This you have always done, and we must all ever strive to keep the Union worthy of the brave men who sacrificed, suffered and died for it. I will be glad, my comrades, to meet you all personally." (Loud cheering and applause.)

At the conclusion of the address, and the demonstration that followed, an informal reception was held. The old veterans filed up to the porch, and extended the hand of fellowship—and some of them only had one hand to give. They were all happy with the bright inspirations of the visit, which came to an end, all too soon, at six o'clock.

A CONTEST FOR PRINCIPLE.

Among the messages received by Major McKinley, Monday morning, June 20th, was a letter from the Young Men's Republican Club of Omaha, Nebraska, saying:

"To the Hon. William McKinley, Canton, Ohio. The Young Men's Republican Club of Omaha, sends greeting to the standard bearer of the Republican party, and gives him assurance that the nomination of a citizen of Nebraska, by the Democratic National Convention will in no wise affect the enthusiasm and the loyalty of the young Republicans of Omaha. This is a contest of principles, and in this contest we shall fight for the triumph of William McKinley, who stands for National honor and National prosperity.

Charles E. Winter, *President.*
James A Beck, *Secretary.*

ENTHUSIASTIC, ACTIVE AND CONFIDENT.

Also the following:

York, Nebraska, July 20, 1896.

"Hon. William McKinley, Canton, Ohio: Notwithstanding Nebraska is the center of the Populistic maelstrom, Republicans are enthusiastic, active and confident. York has a McKinley Club of 525 members, which includes 106 old soldiers. The Club sends its compliments to its great leader, the next President of the United States. Nebraska Republicans are not alarmed nor intimidated; they have fearlessly faced and combatted Populistic vagaries for six years.

N. V. Harlan, *President.*

FOUNDERS' DAY IN THE FOREST CITY.

Major McKinley left Canton on July 22nd for the first time since his nomination for President. He went to Cleveland to attend the opening exercises of the Cleveland Centennial Celebration on Founders' Day, or the hundredth anniversary of the city's first settlement. His appearance in the city created the greatest enthusiasm, and as he passed along the line of the great parade, which was witnessed by fully 250,000 people, there were constant demonstrations in his honor. His address on this occasion was as follows:

49

Major McKinley's Response.

"Mr. PRESIDENT AND MY FELLOW CITIZENS: The people of Cleveland do well to celebrate the hundredth anniversary of their great and beautiful city. Its original builders are long since gone, and their mighty struggles are passing from individual recollection into the field of tradition and history. Anniversaries like this increase our pride for the men who wrought so excellently, despite their trials and hardships, from which the present generation would intuitively shrink. They recall to our minds the high character and courage, the lofty aims and great sacrifices of our sturdy ancestors, and inspire us to revere their memories and imitate their virtues. The thoughtful observance of an anniversary like this, therefore, does all who are associated with it, or who come within its influence, positive good. It unfolds the past and enlightens the present, and by emphasizing the value of the ties of family, home and country, it encourages civic pride and appeals to the highest and best sentiments of our hearts and lives. We have brought to our minds the picture of the beginning and the little we then possessed, in vivid contrast with the much that has been acquired and accomplished since. And if the lesson is rightly learned, it suggests to all of us how much we have to do to contribute our share to the progress and civilization of the future. It is a counting of the sheaves garnered in the harvest of the past, and a stimulus to higher endeavor in the future. A hundred years of effort and sacrifice, of skill and activity, of industry and economy are placed before our eyes. To-day the present generation pays its homage to Cleveland's founders, and offers in her own proud strength and beauty a generous and unqualified testimonial to their wisdom and work. (Applause.) The statistics of the population of Cleveland, and of her growth, production and wealth, do not and can not tell the story of her greatness. We have been listening to the interesting and eloquent words of historian, poet and orator, graphically describing her rise from obscurity to prominence. They have woven into perfect and pleasing narrative the truthful and yet well established record of her advancement from an unknown frontier settlement in the Western wilderness to the proud rank of eleventh city in the United States, the grandest country in the world. (Applause.) We have heard with just pride, so marvellous has been her progress, that among the greatest cities on the earth only sixty-two now outrank Cleveland in population. (Applause.) Her life is as one century to twenty compared with some of that number, yet her civilization is as far advanced as that of the proudest metropolis in the world. (Applause.) In point of government, education, morals, and business thrift and enterprise, Cleveland may well claim recognition with the foremost, and is fairly entitled to warm congratulations and high eulogy on this her Centennial Day. Nor will any envy her people a season of self gratulation and rejoicing. You inaugurate to-day a centennial celebration in honor of your successful past, and its beginning is, with singular appropriateness, called Founders' Day. We have heard with interest, the description of the commercial importance of this city, a port on a chain of lakes whose tonnage and commerce surpass those of any other sea or ocean on the globe. We realize the excellence and superiority of the great railroad systems which center in Cleveland. We marvel at the volume and variety of your numerous manufactories, and see about us, on every hand, the pleasant evidences of your comfort and culture, not only in your beautiful and hospitable homes, but in your churches, schools, charities, factories, business houses, streets and viaducts, public parks, statues and monuments—

Indeed, in your conveniences, adornments and improvements of every sort, we behold all the advantages and blessings of the model, modern city, worthy to be both the pride of a great State and much grander Nation. (Great applause.) This is the accomplishment of a century. Who wrought it—who made all this possible? Whence came they, and what manner of men and women were they to undertake to reclaim the wilderness from its primeval savagery? Such are the questions that come instinctively to our lips. We are told that the original band of fifty pioneers, under the leadership of MOSES CLEVELAND, arrived at the mouth of the Cuyahoga on July 22, 1796, and that they ascended the bank and beheld the beautiful plain, covered with luxuriant forests, which they properly defined as 'a splendid site for a city.' Perhaps the historian can remember the names of a dozen, or discover among us as many of their immediate descendants as there were original settlers, but whether we can call them all or any of them by name, or not, this we do know—they were men of pure lives, nobly consecrated to the good of the community. Sober, serious, even stern and austere they may have been, but grand was their mission and well did they accomplish it. (Applause.) They planted here in the wilderness, upon firm and enduring foundations, the institutions of free government. (Applause.) They recognized and enforced the glorious doctrines and priceless privileges of civil and religious liberty, of law and order, of the rights, dignity and independence of labor, of the rights of property, and of the inviolability of public faith and honor. (Applause.) Never were any men more zealous in patriotic devotion to free government and the Union of the States. On their long and toilsome journey from their Connecticut homes they did not forget the Fourth of July, and, though in sad straits, they celebrated it with thankfulness and joy, and unfurled to the breeze our glorious old flag, with its thirteen stars and stripes, on the Nation's natal day, on its now far distant twentieth anniversary. (Great applause.) They believed not only in the Declaration of Independence, but in the Constitution which gave effect and force to its immortal truths (applause); and no men anywhere struggled more bravely to sustain its great principles than some of these very settlers. (Applause.) Indeed, the tribute which WASHINGTON had paid but a few years before to the men who had settled at the mouth of the Miskingum may well be applied to the little band that founded the Forest City. 'No colony in America,' said he, 'was ever settled under such favorable auspices. Information, prosperity, and strength will be its characteristics. There never were men better calculated to promote the welfare of any community.' They were of the same ancestral stock, of like education and training, and had gained a similar high reputation for ability and energy. Their ideas of government and of the value and importance of education were drawn from the same sources, while their religious faith and sense of justice were also similar. They may frequently have been discouraged, but they were always brave and determined. Their faith was sublime. They were of the stock which gave to the world a civilization without a parallel in recorded history, and offered to the struggling races of men everywhere assurances of the realization of their best and highest aspirations. (Applause.) They opened the door to the oppressed in every land, and the wisdom of their foresight has been abundantly verified by the infusion into our society of those strong and sturdy foreign elements which have given to the Republic so many of its best and patriotic citizens, by whose aid this State and city have become so great. (Applause.) Every step in your advancement is but the confirmation of the wisdom of the fathers, of their foresight and keen sagacity. (Applause.) Your progress and prosperity is their highest testimonial, their most lasting memorial. Glorious pioneer, he made and left his impress wherever he pitched his camp or raised his cabin! (Applause.) His was the impress of the sturdy manhood that feared God and loved liberty. (Applause.) He stands as the representative of a great age and well improved opportunity, 'the sturdiest oak in the great forest of man.' (Applause.) 'As the peak which first catches the morning light is the grand monarch of the hills,' so the sturdy pioneer who struck the first blow for freedom is the grand monarch of our civilization. (Great applause.) Let me commend you to his precious example. It is richer than titles of royalty. (Applause.) God grant that the fires of liberty which he kindled; that the respect for law and order which he inculcated; that the freedom of conscience and religious liberty which he taught, and which found expression in the Constitution of the United States; that the public credit and honor which he established 'as the most important source of our strength and security;' and that the fervent and self-sacrificing devotion to our splendid free institutions, which were ever the animating and controlling purposes of his nature, may be as dear to the people of this and each succeeding generation as they were to him." (Great and long continued applause.)

MAJOR McKINLEY AT ALLIANCE.

The city of Alliance will long remember Thursday, July 23, 1896, as one of the notable days in her history. The semi-centennial of Mt. Union College attracted a large crowd, and the announcement that Major McKinley would attend brought thousands more from all the country round about. He reached Alliance from Cleveland on the Cleveland and Pittsburg Railroad at 9:30 o'clock, and was taken at once to Mt. Union College. As he entered the hall the vast crowd assembled arose, and led by Bishop Vincent, gave him the Chautauqua salute. This was followed by a round of cheers, and then Hon. Lewis Miller, of Akron, introduced him, and he spoke as follows:

Major McKinley's Response.

Mr. President, Members of the Faculty and Students of Mt. Union College, and My Fellow Citizens: It gives me very great pleasure as your neighbor, and as a member of the Board of Trustees of this college to be present with you on this your semi-centennial anniversary. This old institution has a proud history, and I can not stand in your presence to-day without having come to my mind and lips names which are familiar to all who know its career. The venerable founder of the institution, Dr. E. A. Hartshorn, is on the platform. (Applause.) I remember many of his early struggles for the establishment of this seat of learning. Some of his associates in the original work are still with you, and I do not know anywhere in the world more self-sacrificing and more devoted instructors than the former and present faculty of Mt. Union College. (Great Applause.) What a splendid work this institution has done! Everywhere I go, in every State and Territory of the Union, I find members of the Alumni Association of Mt. Union College, and wherever I find them I hear them classed as among the best citizens of the communities in which they reside. (Cheers and applause.) You not only educate men and women here, but you give what is more priceless than education—you give character to men and women. I have come this morning, violating a rule which I had established for myself, that I might mingle with you on this joyous day of jubilee, your fiftieth anniversary. The value of university education can not be overestimated. Its support can not be too generous, nor too earnest, upon the part of our people. But, after all, my fellow citizens, the hope of the Republic, its safety and security, and the strength and perpetuity of popular government must rest upon the great public school system now happily and firmly established throughout the United States. (Great applause.) Nothing can take its place; and, fortunately, the public school is everywhere becoming the vestibule of the university. As the curriculum of the free school is advanced the tie between fundamental and higher education is closer and stronger, and is more clearly recognized and appreciated. We can not have too much education if it be of the right kind; and if it be rightly applied it is of inestimable value to the citizen in every walk and profession of life. Young men and women, what your education will be and do for you depends upon yourselves. The chief difference in men, in school or out, is in the amount of work they do. No measure of genius, so called, will take the place of well directed, hard work. It is not so much what is in the course of studies at college which does you good, as it is what you master there. The mental discipline, and the application of what you learn, is the aim of real education. The acquisition of learning is useless unless it is put to some wise end in the practical affairs of life. The young man who has received only an elementary training is at a disadvantage compared with his rival who has received a higher education. This is evident from the ease and dexterity with which the one successfully disposes of problems that the other wrestles with, perhaps unavailingly, for hours or days at a stretch. The need of the times is thorough education, thorough equipment for life's work; and that man succeeds best who is practical, sensible and broad, who really knows the most, has the best stored mind, and knows best how to use it. Do not permit college ideals to warp you nor to remove you from active participation in the every day affairs of life. You have something to do, every one of you, in this active world. Fortunately for the United States, the founders of the Government clearly foresaw that the perpetuity of our institutions could be secured only by making ample provision for popular education. They realized far better than we do, that without learning there could be no real liberty, and that the one could not be enjoyed without the other. (Applause.) To my mind the most wonderful work of the fathers, second only to union and independence, was the broad, wise and enduring provisions they made for public instruction. No country in the world is so well provided with educational advantages; no colleges in any other land have bestowed upon them such munificent gifts as the educational institutions of the United States. (Applause.) By the Ordinance of the Congress of the Confederation in 1785, Section 16 (a square mile) of every township was reserved for the maintenance of public schools. The Ordinance of 1787 confirmed the Ordinance of 1785, and declared that 'religion, morality and knowledge, being necessary to good government and the happiness of mankind, schools, and the means of education, shall be forever encouraged.' In contemplating this Ordinance I marvel at the supreme sagacity of its authors. The people, and especially the youth of the present day, little comprehend the importance and grandeur of this great act, as it relates to education alone. It was without precedent or suggestion in the previous legislation of mankind. Even its framers could have but faintly conceived the immensity of the domain and the value of the boon they were conferring upon posterity. It is without parallel among the great acts of patriotism which the grand men of that age were constantly performing. Priceless heritage to American youth, it has exerted an influence most benign upon every State since organized! Especially the great States of the North-west, whose school systems and schools are to-day probably the best in the world. (Applause.) In them is found the most perfect union between the elementary and advanced schools, from the kindergarten to the university, ever known or attempted by any country, with abundant means for the sup-port of all from the lowest to the highest. The total amount of money realized from this munificent grant can not be accurately stated, but enough is known to warrant the estimate that it is now not less than one hundred million dollars. In referring to this great Ordinance I love to recall the words of Webster. They can not be repeated too frequently, nor become too familiar to the pupils of this and of every generation. You will remember that he said: 'We are accustomed to praise the lawgivers of antiquity, we help to perpetuate the fame of Solon and Lycurgus, but I doubt whether one single law of any lawgiver, ancient or modern, has produced effects of a more distinct, marked and lasting character than the Ordinance of 1787. We see its consequences at this moment, and we shall never cease to see them, perhaps, while the Ohio shall flow. It fixed forever the character of the population in the vast region northwest of the Ohio.' The spirit of this Ordinance found lodgment in the Constitution, and the words and acts of the fathers can not fail to instruct and inspire the people of every age in American history. Enlightened citizenship was to the fathers the great essential to every State and community. Washington, in his Farewell Address, gave utterance to these wise admonitions, which are as applicable to the people of to-day as they were to the people of the Revolutionary period. He said: 'Promote, as an object of primary importance, institutions for the general diffussion of knowledge. In proportion as the structure of a government gives force to public opinion, it is essential that public opinion should be enlightened.' We must not forget that one great aim and object of education is to elevate the standard of citizenship. The uplifting of our schools will undoubtedly result in a higher and better tone in business and professional life. Old methods and standards may be good, but they must advance with the new problems and needs of the of the age. This age demands an education which, while not depreciating in any degree the inestimable advantages of high intellectual culture, shall best fit the man and woman for his her or calling, whatever it may be. Character is the foundation upon which we must build if our institutions are to endure. Our obligations for the splendid advantages we enjoy should not rest upon us too lightly. We owe to our country much. We must give in return for these matchless educational opportunities the best results in our lives. (Applause.) We must make our citizenship worthy the great Republic, intelligent, patriotic, and self-sacrificing, or our institutions will fail of their high purpose, and our civilization will inevitably decline. Our hope is in good education and good morals. Let us fervently pray that our educational institutions may always be generously supported, and that those who go out from these halls will be themselves the best witnesses of their force and virtue in popular government." (Great applause.)

SPEECH ON THE CAMPUS.

But the crowd assembled was far in excess of the capacity of the hall. Those who could not gain admission waited outside to greet Major McKINLEY, the guest of honor of the day. His appearance was the signal for an outburst of applause, and the great throng began to call for a speech. The distinguished guest smilingly demurred until the outcry was so great that he was obliged to raise his hand for silence, and thank them for their kind reception—speaking as follows:

"My FELLOW CITIZENS: I am very glad indeed to have the pleasure of meeting my old friends and constituents of Stark, Columbiana and Mahoning Counties. I am glad to know that 1896 is to be a year of patriotism and dedication to country. (Applause.) I am glad to know that the people all over the country this year mean to be devoted to one flag, and that the glorious old Stars and Stripes (applause); that the people this year mean to maintain the financial honor of the Nation as sacredly as they would maintain the honor of the flag. (Cheering and applause.) I am glad to meet and greet you all this morning, and I would be pleased to talk longer to you, but for an engagement which takes me to Cleveland. I thank you all and bid you good-bye." (Great applause.)

TO ALLIANCE WORKINGMEN.

At the Alliance station, where his train was surrounded by the employes of the Morgan Engineering Company, the Steel Works, and hundreds of other citizens, Major McKINLEY spoke as follows:

"My FELLOW CITIZENS: I am very grateful for this unexpected call and greeting. For more than a quarter of a century I have been in the habit of coming to the city of Alliance, meeting her people and conferring with them touching public questions of great individual and National concern. I am here to-day to attend the fiftieth anniversary of Mt. Union College, and I only appear now that I may acknowledge the kind welcome which you have so generously given me. (Applause.) All of us are interested in the welfare of our country, because in the welfare of our country is involved the individual welfare of every citizen. If our great country is prosperous then the people are prosperous. What we want, no matter to what political organization we may have belonged in the past, is a return of the good times of four years ago. We want good prices and good wages, and when we shall have them again we want them paid in good money. (Applause and cries of 'You are right.') Whether our prices be high or low, whether our wages be good or bad, they are all better by being paid in dollars worth one hundred cents each. (Tremendous cheering.) If we have good wages, they are better by being paid in good dollars. If we have poor wages, they are made poorer by being paid in poor dollars. What we all want more than anything else is to keep our money equal to that of the most enlightened nations of the earth and maintain unsullied the credit, the honor, and the good faith of the Government of the United States. (Great applause.) We are the greatest country in the world—greatest in our freedom, greatest in our opportunities, greatest in our possibilities—and we are too great to taint our country's honor or to cast suspicion on the credit or the obligations of our Government. (Applause.) I thank you, my fellow citizens, and especially you, my friends, the workingmen of Alliance, who have left your shops and factories to attest your interest in the great political contest now pending, for let me tell you that I believe no higher compliment could be paid to any cause than to have the support of the men who toil. (Applause.) I thank you all and bid you good-bye."

Then ensued another great demonstration, the workingmen crowding about Major McKinley and repeatedly cheering him. He greeted all cordially, shaking hands with hundreds, and calling many by name, until at 11:40 his train pulled out for Cleveland.

THE NEW ENGLAND DINNER.

New England Day was celebrated at Cleveland on the campus of Adelbert College, on Wednesday, July 23d, and there Major McKinley was given another most flattering reception, and prevailed upon to make his fourth speech of the morning and afternoon. He was hailed with rapturous applause, and spoke as follows:

"Mr. President and Ladies and Gentlemen: It gives me sincere pleasure to meet and address for a moment the New England Society of the city of Cleveland and Western Reserve of Ohio. Those of us who are not descendants of the Pilgrims of New England join cheerfully with those who are to pay high tribute to the men who did so much for civilization and for the establishment of free government on this continent. (Applause.) There has been every variety of characterization of the New England pilgrim and pioneer—some of it of a friendly nature, but far too much of it captious, harsh and unjust. At this moment the picture of the Puritan painted by that gifted son of New England, the late George William Curtis, whose memory we revere and will ever cherish, rises before me. (Applause.) He said that the Puritan was 'narrow, bigoted, sour, hard and intolerant, but he was the man whom God had sifted three kingdoms to find as the seed-grain wherewith to plant a free Republic,' and that he had 'done more for liberty than any man in human history.' It is said that the blood of New England courses through the veins of a quarter of the population of the United States. I know not how this may be, but I do know that the ideas, principles and the conscience of New England course though every vein and artery of the American Republic. (Cheers and applause.) Well may you be proud to be descended from New England people, for never was anything more happily said of them than these words by Whittier:

'No lack was in thy primal stock,
No weakling founders builded here;
They were the men of Plymouth Rock—
The Huguenot and the Cavalier.'

The Puritan has fought—aye, and died—on every battle-field of the Republic from Concord and Bunker Hill to Gettysburg and Appomattox. (Great applause.) And the torch of liberty he lit still illumines the whole world. I bid you, again in the language of our beloved Whittier,—

'Hold fast to your Puritan heritage;—
But let the free light of the age,
Its life, its hope, its sweetness add
To the sterner faith your fathers had.'

(Great cheering.)

THE WINDOW GLASS WORKERS OF AMERICA.

The streets of Canton were filled with marching people Saturday morning, July 25th, when the eight hundred delegates of the Window Glass Workers' Association of North America came to pay their respects to their esteemed friend and champion, WILLIAM MCKINLEY. The delegates had been in attendance at the eighth annual National Convention of the Association in Pittsburg and concluded it would be a fitting way to close their session by paying him a visit. The delegation arrived at 10:40 via the Ft. Wayne railroad on a special train of eleven coaches. They were met at the depot by the Canton Troop, and the First Ward Drum Corps, and, headed by the Select Knight's Band, of Pittsburg, they marched to Major MCKINLEY's residence. When the column reached the house the band rendered a patriotic selection, and while awaiting the appearance of Major MCKINLEY the Glee Club of twenty members sang several campaign airs which were heartily cheered. When Major MCKINLEY appeared in the midst of the Committee he was received with a great demonstration of applause from all present, during which Mr. HENRY BOSTICK, a delegate from Princeton, Indiana, climbed upon a chair, and as soon as silence was restored, spoke as follows:

"Major MCKINLEY: I have been delegated by the Committee representing my fellow workmen, the delegates to the Eighth National Convention of Window Glass Workers of North America, to present them to you, and the sentiments I express are such as I have been instructed to express by this Committee, consisting of JAMES CAMPBELL, G. L. CAKE, GEORGE AMBOS, JOHN T. MORGAN, HENRY BOSTICK and JOHN P. EBERHART. The men who stand before you to-day have come from the States ranging from the Berkshire hills in Massachusetts to the broad prairies of Illinois, and from the Great Lakes to beyond Mason and Dixon's line. From eleven States we come, representing the overwhelming majority sentiment of all our fellow workmen who toil in the great window glass industry in every factory in the United States. We come fresh from the exacting school of experience. Our people have seen the tariff reduced in 1846, and that they suffered a reduction in wages in consequence. Another reduction of the tariff occurred in 1857, with a like reduction in our wages. The tariff was increased in 1861, and our wages were accordingly advanced. Again in 1890 the tariff was advanced, and we received a corresponding benefit. In 1893 the Gorman-Wilson Bill was passed, destroying the protective features of the then existing McKinley Law, and greatly reducing the tariff, and we were in consequence not only greatly reduced in the rate of wages received for a given amount of work, but were thrown into a state of idleness, hunger and hardship. We come then to greet you whom that experience has taught us to regard as the only inflexible, unbending and universally recognized champion of the very cornerstone of American progress—protection to home industries. Its effects are general and advantageous to every class of American citizen. To the farmer, by making dutiable the imports of such foreign products as meet like home products in the American markets, and by creating through the general operations of the policy, an active, reliable and remunerative market for all his products; to the employer who uses his capital in operating manufacturing enterprises, by creating and maintaining an active and healthy market for his wares, insuring to him through an increased ability of the people to buy and use his wares, an active and steady demand, and hence a reliable activity in business; and for the laborer who toils in the employer's shops, by insuring him steady employment at fair wages, with all the attendant blessings and privileges of working and living as citizens of this great and wonderfully resourceful country should be privileged to work and live--for we know that an increased development of and production from our natural resources, if coupled with the multiplied consumption of the product by our own people, must inevitably exert a refining influence on our American civilization, and tend to elevate the standard of American citizenship, which can never rise higher than the average of the intelligence, morality and manhood of the whole people. We love our country and have confidence in our Government. We believe that its immense wealth, phenomenal resources, the loyalty and bravery of its sons, the intelligence and genius of its people, all based upon and nurtured by the beneficent influence of its free institutions, insure it against destruction or serious hurt from invasion with the sword by any foreign foe, but our experience has taught us that the invasion of our markets by the cheap labor of Europe is dangerous and destructive to the very foundations of our liberties, and constitutes a foe to our institutions in all that makes them truly free and distinctly American, inasmuch as they are based upon and can be maintained only by a care for the education of our children up to a high and intelligent citizenship. (Applause.) We believe that the only power that can successfully meet and render the invasion of this natural foe harmless is the operation of that great bulwark of American prosperity, the protective principle, strictly adhered to in the levying of duties on the importation of foreign products, which principle we believe to have been most ably and fully enunciated in the provisions of that wisely conservative and patriotic measure, the McKinley Law, of which we recognize you as the great architect who planned and builded it, schedule by schedule, and inaugurated that grand system that spoke out hope and prosperity to the people and all the people of this Nation. We want that principle restored to the statutes. We are satisfied with the quality of our dollars, and have no fear about the volume of our money as a Nation, if the tariff is so regulated, and levied on such principles, as to protect American industries, and provide sufficient funds to meet the ordinary expenses of the Government, thereby insuring to us the opportunity to work and receive the money that is the just reward of an American workingman. At the same time we demand that if the employers in foreign countries would bring the products of their cheap labor to compete in our markets with the products of our free American labor, they must meet us on even ground by bringing back with those products some of the gold that the present Administration has been forced first to borrow, and then return to them as interest on the public debt—a debt they are steadily increasing, and rendering more burdensome, day by day, as they proceed. All, or nearly all of this, is through the operations of their great panacea, 'Tariff Reform,' sometimes called 'Tariff for Revenue Only,' which we would amend by changing the punctuation and adding a few words, making it read, 'Tariff for Revenue, Only it Fails to Produce the Revenue.' (Cheers.) We desired to greet you personally, Major McKINLEY, because we look upon you as the favorite son of the United States, not the choice of any political machine, or urged by the people within the confines of a single State; but the one to whom the people all looked when they began to realize that the time had come when a standard bearer must be chosen as a candidate of a great party for President of the United States—the one whose name spontaneously burst from the care and sorrow-burdened hearts of the American people—the one grand character round whom every humble home and hearthstone in our broad land was clustering its hopes and are still clinging its faith for better and brighter days. We greet you, then, as our ideal of American citizenship, the unassuming soldier, patriot and statesman, the hope of our people and the next President of the United States." (Tremendous cheering.)

Major McKinley's Response.

"Mr. BOSTICK AND WINDOWGLASS WORKERS OF THE UNITED STATES: It is peculiarly gratifying to me to have this large body of the representatives of your Association, fresh from your deliberative Convention, and speaking for your great industry scattered over eleven States of the Union, honor me with a call of greeting and congratulation. I appreciate the words of confidence so eloquently expressed by your spokesman and agree with him that there is something fundamentally wrong about our governmental affairs that demands a speedy remedy, which can only be had by the people speaking through the constitutional forms at the next general election. (Great applause.) You have spoken of some of our difficulties with singular force and accuracy, demonstrating that you appreciate fully the great problems which are before the people for investigation and settlement. Nothing could be better said than that a great essential to the credit of the country is to provide enough revenue to run the country. The credit of any government is imperiled so long as it expends more money than it collects. The credit of the government, like that of the individual citizen, is best subserved by living within its means, and providing means with which to live. Every citizen must know, as you have stated, that the receipts of the United States are now insufficient for its necessary expenditures, and that our present revenue laws have resulted in causing a deficiency in the Treasury for almost three years. It has been demonstrated, too, that no relief can be had through the present Congress. The relief rests with the people themselves. (Cheers.) They are charged with the election of a new Congress in November, which alone can give the needed relief. If they elect a Republican Congress, the whole world knows that one of its first acts will be to put upon the statute books of the country a law under which the Government will collect enough money to meet its expenditures, stop debts and deficiencies, and adequately protect American labor. (Great cheering and applause.) This would be one of the surest steps toward the return of confidence and a revival of business prosperity. (Applause.) The Government, my fellow citizens, has not been the only sufferer in the past three years, as your spokesman has vividly shown. The people have suffered, the laboring man in his work and wages, the farmer in his prices and markets, and our citizens generally in their incomes and investments. Enforced idleness among the people has brought to many American homes gloom and wretchedness, where cheer and hope once dwelt. Both Government and people have paid dearly for a mistaken policy, a policy which has disturbed our industries and· cut down our revenues, always so essential to our credit, independence and prosperity. Having stricken down our industries, a new experiment is now proposed, one that would debase our currency and further weaken, if not wholly destroy, public confidence. Workingmen, have we not had enough of such rash and costly experiments? (Cries of 'We have! We have!') Don't all of us wish for the return of the economic policy which for more than a third of a century gave the Government its highest credit and the citizen his greatest prosperity? (Great applause and cries of 'Yes,' 'Yes.') As four years ago the people were warned against the industrial policy proclaimed by our political adversaries, which has since brought ruin upon the country, and were entreated to reject the theories which actual trial had always shown to be fraught with disaster to our revenues, employments and enterprises, so now they are again warned to reject this new remedy, no matter by what party or leaders it may be offered, as certain to entail upon the country only increased and aggravated disaster and suffering, and bring no good or profit to any public interest whatever. (Applause.) Circumstances have given to the Republican party at this juncture of our National affairs a place of supreme duty and responsibility. Seldom, if ever, has any political party occupied a post of such high importance as that entrusted to the Republican party this year. Indeed, it may be confidently asserted that never before has any political organization been so clearly and conspicuously called to do battle for so much that is best in government than is this year demanded of the Republican party. But, happily, it will not contend alone. It will number among its allies, friends and supporters, thousands of brave, patriotic and conscientious political opponents of the past, who will join our ranks and make common cause in resisting the proposed debasement of our currency and the degradation of our country's honor,—earnest and strong men who will strive as zealously as we for the triumph of correct principles and the continued supremacy of law and order, those strongest and mightiest pillars of free government. (Great applause.) The determination of this contest calls for the exercise of the gravest duty of good citizenship, and partisanship should not weigh against patriotism, as, indeed, I am very sure that it will not, in the calm and proper settlement of the questions which confront us. The whole country rejoices to-day that the strong and sturdy men who toil are enlisted in the cause of American honor, American patriotism, American production and American prosperity—a cause which must surely win before the great tribunal of the American people. (Tremendous applause.) I thank you, my fellow citizens, for the compliment of this call, and your manifestations of personal regard and good will, and it will give me sincere pleasure to meet each of you personally." (Loud and long continued applause.)

CHICAGO UNIVERSITY REPUBLICAN CLUB.

The Committee which called at his residence, Wednesday afternoon, July 29th, to present to Major McKinley a bust of himself, modeled by the famous sculptor Hans Hirsh, was received in the parlor. A party of newspaper men and several personal friends of Major McKinley attended when the presentation was made by Mr. J. C. Ickes in behalf of the Republican Club of Chicago University. The gift came as a token of the high appreciation of the students of the University for Major McKinley, and Mr. Ickes said:

"Major McKinley: The eyes of all America are just now turned toward Canton as the City of Hope whence is to come forth the champion who is to save his country from the heresies which threaten her. Already a number of wise men have come out of the East to see this new prophet who has arisen, and they have spread abroad such reports of his might and power that our hearts have prompted us to see for ourselves. With this purpose in view we have traveled from afar out of the boundless West and we rejoice to find our hopes more than realized. We come as the representatives of the host of young Republicans who are enrolled in our colleges to-day; we come because we are patriotic and because the modern college man takes an especial interest in all that pertains to the welfare of his country. We all love WILLIAM McKINLEY and all that his name stands for in the present great crisis of our National life. (Applause.) We often hear it said that there is nothing in a name, but I can repeat to you a name that means honor, sincerity and truth, a name that has already been written in history among the noblest and best men that our country has produced, a name that is to receive still greater fame and glory in the future. I refer to the Republican nominee for President of the United States—WILLIAM McKINLEY. (Applause.) Major McKinley, in behalf of the Republican Club of the University of Chicago, it is my privilege to present to you this masterpiece of a great artist, a masterpiece not only because of its perfection, but because of him whom it represents, hoping that you will accept it in the spirit in which it is offered—a spirit of profound love and esteem." (Applause.)

Major McKinley's Response.

"MR. ICKES AND GENTLEMEN: It gives me great pleasure to meet this Committee from the Republican Club of the University of Chicago, and I can but say that if the Republican party is to continue its progress of power and usefulness, it must be done through the conscience and intelligence of the people. It is indeed a good omen to find the young gentlemen of the many colleges of the United States attaching themselves to the Republican organizations to sustain correct political principles and the National honor. (Applause.) There is no class of men more potent than those who go out from the colleges into every county and State of the Union. They wield a mighty power, and it is fortunate for the country that so many of them are enlisted this year for the principles of good government and clean political methods, an honest canvass and a pure and intelligent civil service. (Applause.) I am glad to know that Republican principles are such that they can be submitted with safety and confidence to the intelligence of the educated men of the country. I am pleased with the bust which you have been so kind as to bring me, and I accept it in the spirit in which it has been presented. I beg that you convey to the artist and members of the Republican Club of the University of Chicago my sincere thanks for it." (Applause.)

THE KNOXVILLE McKINLEY AND HOBART CLUB.

The McKinley and Hobart Club, of Knoxville, Pa., a suburb of Pittsburg, accompanied by a number of friends, came to pay their respects to Major McKINLEY on Thursday, July 30th. It was a fine delegation, numbering some five hundred men, thoroughly representative of a great State, coming from farm, forge, shop and store, and, in the words of the spokesman, "representing that hive of industry—that mighty workshop—composed of Pittsburg and her neighboring borough." The delegation was well organized and marched like a regiment of regulars. A band headed the procession and a quartet styled the "Tariff League Singers of Pittsburg," accompanied the Club. Mr. JOHN P. EBERHARD, President of the McKinley and Hobart Club, who is also President of the Glass Workers' Union, acted as spokesman for the visitors. He said:

"Major McKINLEY: We come from that wonderful hive of industry, that mighty workshop, composed of Pittsburg and its neighboring boroughs. We are

Republicans, and we believe in our party and its principles. We are proud of its record and the result of its policy in the past; and we have faith in that party as being the only medium through which we may hope for a return of prosperity to the people, both in the agricultural and manufacturing industries of the whole country. We believe in bimetalism, and we recognize in the Republican party the only real, true and safe advocate of that policy, namely, the use of both gold and silver as money, each interchangeable with the other, each dollar as good as every other dollar. We do not, and we feel assured that you do not, believe in monometalism, or the use of either gold or silver as the only money; and knowing this, we know you will and must oppose the visionary ideas of those who would seek to create values by the legislative fiat of the Nation, and the attempts of those who seek to place us upon the single silver basis, thereby driving our gold out of circulation and out of the country. We believe you will use all the power you possess as the Chief Executive of the United States to bring about, by international agreement, which is the only manner in which it can be accomplished, the restoration of silver as a money metal at a fixed ratio with gold. We believe, sir, that wise legislation, on the principle of protection, and to the end that it will yield an abundant revenue for the expenses of the Government, for the payment of debts, for the improvement of our rivers and harbors, for the upbuilding of our navy, and for internal improvements of various kinds will restore our country to great prosperity and will solve the money problem about which so many of our people seem to be concerned. We recognize in your public career and in your private life those noble qualities of mind and heart that give us the assurance that the great interests of this country, over which you will shortly be called to preside, will be in safe hands, and that you, trusting in the strength and guided by the counsels of the Supreme Ruler of nations, will be able to discharge the grave responsibility and execute the duties of your high office so as to lead us as a people in the higher paths of duty to more glorious achievements than have marked our wonderful past." (Applause.)

Major McKinley's Response.

After the storm of applause which greeted Major McKinley had subsided, he said:

"Mr. Eberhard and My Fellow Citizens: I am glad, indeed, to meet and greet the Knoxville McKinley and Hobart Club in this city and at my home, and I thank you cordially for traveling so long a distance to express your personal good will to me and your devotion to the great principles of the Republican party. You are right, Mr. Spokesman, in saying that the Republican party stands now, as it has always stood, for a sound and stable currency and for the maintenance of all its money of every kind at parity, so that it shall always be equal to the best money of the most civilized nations of the earth. (Applause.) A depreciated currency, as you have so well said, would work disaster to the interests of the people, and to none more than those of the workingmen and farmers. Long years ago Daniel Webster said that those who were the least able to bear it were the first to feel it and the last to recover from it. 'A disordered currency,' said he, 'is fatal to industry, frugality, and economy. It fosters the spirit of speculation and extravagance. It is the most effectual of inventions to fertilize the rich man's fields with the sweat of the poor man's brow.' That which we call money, my fellow citizens, and with which values are measured and settlements made, must be as true as the bushel which measures the grain of the farmer, and as honest as the hours of labor which the man who toils is required to give. (Loud applause.) The one must be as full and complete and as honest as the other. (Applause.) Our currency to-day is good—all of it is as good as gold and has been so ever since the Republican party secured the resumption of specie payments in 1879—and it is the unfaltering determination of the Republican party to so keep and maintain it forever. (Cheers.) It is the duty of the people of this country to stand unitedly against every effort to degrade our currency or debase our credit. (Cries of 'They will.') They must unite now as they have united in the past in every great crisis of our country's history without regard to past party affiliations or differences to uphold the National credit and honor as sacredly as our flag. (Cheers.) When the country seemed wildly bent on inflation in the years preceding the resumption of specie payments the sober sense of the American people without regard to party united and stemmed that threatened tide of irredeemable paper money and repudiation and placed and kept the Nation on the rock of public honor, sound finance, and honest currency. You have rightly stated that the Republican party not only believes in sound money and the highest public faith and honor on the part of the Government of the United States to all its creditors, but also that it believes in a tariff which while raising enough money to conduct the Government, economically administered, will serve the highest and best interests of American labor, American agriculture, American commerce, and American citizenship. (Cheers) Some of our political opponents are given to saying that the tariff question is settled. If we are not wrong in interpreting their meaning, we think they are right, (laughter), and thank them for the confession. (Applause.) We believe that the tariff question is settled—settled in the minds and hearts of the American people, and settled on the side of protection. (Tremendous cheering.) But, however firmly it may be settled in the public mind, it is not yet settled in public law. What is in the hearts and consciences of the people touching any public question is not effective until it is written in public statute, and this can only be done through the elective franchise in the choice of a Congress of the United States, which makes our public laws. No one, I take it, will regard the present tariff law as a just and final settlement of the question. Whatever may be our differences about the economic principle upon which tariff legislation should be made, all agree that the present tariff law is a failure, even as a revenue measure. So, without discussing the principle of free trade or protection, everybody must appreciate that no law is a settlement which creates every month a deficiency in the public treasury. (Loud applause and cheers for 'McKinley.') The people of this country are not satisfied with such an enactment, and will not be satisfied until a public law shall express the public will in a statute which provides adequate revenues for the needs of the Government. full security for its credit, and ample protection to the labor. capital and energy of the American people. (Applause.) I thank you, my fellow citizens, for this friendly call, and I assure you that it will give me pleasure to meet each of you personally."

CAMBRIDGE AND GUERNSEY COUNTY.

Three hundred citizens of Guernsey County visited Canton on Friday morning, July 31, to pay their personal respects to Major McKinley and tender formal congratulations. The delegation was about evenly divided between members of the G. A. R. Posts of Cambridge and employes of the Cambridge tin mill. The party came to this city by way of the C., T. and V. railroad, arrived here at eleven o'clock, and were at once escorted to Major McKinley's residence by George D. Harter and Canton G. A. R. Posts and the McKinley Drum Corps. When they arrived at the McKinley residence after a selection by the O. U. A. M. band of Cambridge, Mr. H. S. Moses, commander of George D. Harter Post, presented Colonel Joseph D. Taylor to Major McKinley as the spokesman for the visitors. He referred to the flood of high water through which their train had come from Cambridge, and said:

"Major McKinley: We come to-day to tender you our personal regards and to add congratulations to the many hitherto given you. We have not come as partisans but as friends and neighbors. You have to-day before you in this delegation many comrades of the G. A. R. of Cambridge. They are men who have learned to love you for your patriotic devotion to your country in time of war and in time of peace. These old comrades have come to pay tribute to your high personal character and for the public service you have rendered. The old soldiers want one thing remembered, and that is that the honor and integrity of the old flag must be maintained. (Cheers.) You heard it said in Congress that we could not make tin in this country but I want to say that we have in this crowd men who are employed in the Cambridge tin mill. They work in a tin mill which has sent out 6,000 tons or 120,000 boxes, of tin a year and it is as good as any tin plate made across the water. (Cheers.) These men have come from Guernsey County, from all the walks of life. We have come to believe that the star of hope for the laboring man is resting in Canton. In behalf of the men and women in this delegation—for there are a number of ladies who have come along with us—I extend greeting to you and Mrs. McKinley." (Applause.)

After the cheering had ended Dr. W. H. McFarland was introduced. He is bowed under the weight of years and as Chaplain of the Ninety-eighth Regiment Ohio Volunteer Infantry is well known throughout the State. He said that he had come to see and hear and grasp the hand once more of the most illustrious friend of labor in the United States. (Cheers.) "He is the man who has done more for the laboring men than any other man in this country—or in the world for that matter. No one has done more to elevate or dignify labor and no man has put a brighter crown of glory on the brow of honest toil than you." (Great applause.)

Major McKinley's Response.

Major McKinley spoke without manuscript, or notes, and with great force and eloquence. He was cheered time and again, and at the conclusion of his address there was the crush of visitors to grasp his hand. He said:

"Colonel Taylor, Dr. McFarland, My Comrades and Fellow Citizens: It gives me great gratification to receive this call from my friends and fellow citizens of Guernsey County, where I have made so many visits in years gone by that I know most of you personally. But aside from that I know something of the quality of your population and the spirit of your people. I know

something of your loyalty and devotion to the Union in war, and I know much
of your loyalty and devotion to good government in peace, (Cheers) and, knowing you as I do, I am certain that neither flood nor fire would stop you from
doing what you had proposed to do. (Laughter and applause.) I am glad to
meet the representatives of labor who are assembled here this morning. I
congratulate them upon the advance that has been made in the tin-plate
industry to which my old colleague in Congress, Col. TAYLOR, has referred. I
am glad to know that Republican legislation gave to this country an industry
which insures work and wages to American workingmen and brings happiness
to American homes. (Great cheering and applause.) I am glad, too, my fellow
citizens, to meet my old comrades of the Grand Army of the Republic,
(applause) my comrades of thirty-five years ago, for the war commenced over
thirty-five years ago, and it is nearly thirty-two years since its close. It seems
not so long, not so far away to us, but as I look into the faces of the old soldiers
before me, I can see that age is stamping its lines of care upon them. Their
steps are no longer as steady and firm as they used to be, but their hearts are just
as loyal to the old flag of the Union as ever. (Tremendous cheering.) They are
just as loyal to National honor to-day as they were loyal to National unity then.
(Applause.) When the war closed there were two great debts resting upon
this Government. One was the debt due to the men who had loaned the
Government money with which to carry on its military operations. The other
debt was due to the men who had willingly offered their lives for the preservation of the American Union. (Cheers.) The old soldiers waited on their
pensions until this great debt of the Government was well out of the way.
They waited patiently until the Government of the United States had paid
nearly two-thirds of that great money debt and refunded it all to a lower rate
of interest. The old soldiers never were in favor of repudiating that debt.
(Applause.) They wanted every dollar of it, principal and interest, paid in the
best coin known to the commercial world; (great applause) and every dollar
of that debt, up to this hour, has been paid in gold, or its equivalent, the recognized best money of the hour, (cheers) and every dollar of that debt, my comrades,
yet to be paid, will be paid in the same unquestioned coin. (Tremendous cheering.) Most of that debt is out of the way. The great debt of this Government now,
is to the surviving soldiers of the Republic. (Applause.) There are 970,000
pensioners on the honored pension roll of this Government to-day, and the
Government pays out of its public treasury in pensions over $140,000,000 every
year to our soldiers and sailors, or their widows and orphans. Every dollar of
that debt must be paid in the best currency and coin of the world. (Great
cheers and cries of "The Republican party will do that.') There is nobody
more interested in maintaining a sound and stable currency than the old
soldiers of the Republic, (applause and cries of 'You are right, Major,') their
widows and their orphans. Our old commander, General GRANT (applause)
whose memory is cherished by all of us, performed two great and conspicious
acts while President of the United States. One was the vetoing of the Inflation
Bill, which would have cast us hopelessly upon a sea of depreciated currency.
The other was the signing of the Resumption Act, for the safe and speedy
resumption of specie payments, which placed every dollar of money upon
the sound foundation of financial honor and unquestioned National honesty,
and the old soldiers this year, as in all the years of the past, following their
Old Commander, will stand by the financial honor of the Government, and
will no more permit their Nation's integrity to be questioned than they
would permit that flag (pointing to an American flag) to be assailed. (Applause

65

and cries of 'You are right.') I thank you, my fellow citizens, for your call and congratulations, and assure you that it will afford me much pleasure to meet each and all of you personally." (Applause and cheers.)

CONGRATULATIONS BY WIRE AND MAIL.

WHILE Major McKINLEY was receiving the personal congratulations of thousands of his fellow citizens in Ohio, the wires were busy conveying him almost as many similar messages from all parts of the Union. Not only was the special wire at his residence carrying him hundreds of friendly greetings from St. Louis, but the telegraph offices in Canton were flooded with messages they could hardly receive much less deliver. The same condition prevailed at Pittsburg, where at one o'clock Friday morning, June 19th, the Western Union Co. reported that there were congratulatory telegrams piled a foot high in their office which it was impossible to transmit. Up to that time several thousand had already been received by Major McKINLEY, the rush beginning before his nomination and continuing for some days after. Among the thousands of messages received, including some that came by mail, were the following:

Hon. Garret A. Hobart, of New Jersey, the Republican nominee for Vice President: "Accept my hearty congratulations and those of the New Jersey delegation." To which Major McKINLEY replied: "I send you my cordial congratulations and hope you can visit me on your way home."

Hon. Thomas B. Reed, of Maine, Speaker of the National House of Representatives: "I wish you a happy and prosperous Administration; happy for yourself and prosperous for the country."

Hon. Matthew S. Quay, U. S. Senator, Beaver, Pennsylvania: "I congratulate you upon the splendid vote of confidence you received from the Convention, which represents the absolute thought of the Republican party of the Nation.

Hon. Levi P. Morton, Governor of New York, Rhinecliff: "You may recall my remark, in 1879, as we sat side by side in the House of Representatives, that I expected some day to see you President of the United States. Please accept to-day my heartiest congratulations."

Hon. William B. Allison, U. S. Senator, Dubuque, Iowa: "Accept my sincere and hearty congratulations upon your nomination."

Hon. William O. Bradley, Governor of Kentucky, Frankfort: "Allow me to extend to you my hearty congratulations on your success. I have no doubt you will be triumphantly elected, and that you will come fully up to the expectations of your friends in the discharge of every duty which may be presented. I was invited to go to Cincinnati to-night for a ratification meeting. But owing to the large accumulation of important business during my absence at the Convention, found it impossible to do so, and so telegraphed. I shall not fail to do my duty in the approaching contest, unless it should be from inability. Kindest wishes for your success."

Hon. Shelby M. Cullom, U. S. Senator, Springfield, Illinois: "Please accept my hearty congratulations for yourself and Mrs. McKinley. You will be triumphantly elected."

Hon. Cushman K. Davis, U. S. Senator, St. Paul, Minnesota: "Permit me to add my congratulations to the many you are receiving. Your nomination is a fulfillment and realization of Republican principles decreed by the people themselves. I feel sure that history will date from that nomination the greatest epoch of prosperity for the American people they have ever enjoyed."

Hon. Charles F. Manderson, Omaha, Nebraska: "Congratulations of Mrs. Manderson and myself on your nomination and certainty of election as President."

Hon. Benjamin Harrison, ex-President of the United States, Indianapolis: "I beg to extend to you my hearty congratulations upon your nomination and to express my confidence that the people will in November ratify the work of the St. Louis Convention. Please present my respects to Mrs. McKinley."

Hon. Whitelaw Reid, New York: "It should be a matter of the greatest personal pride to you that while our party has existed for a quarter of a century there has never before been so good a chance for a square fight and a splendid victory for Protection and Honest Money."

Hon. George L. Wellington, U. S. Senator-elect. Cumberland, Maryland: "Our State will give you eight electoral votes in November."

Hon. Stephen B. Elkins, U. S. Senator, West Virginia: "The people will see to it that your election will follow. West Virginia will be in the McKinley column."

Hon. Henry Cabot Lodge, U. S. Senator, Nahant, Massachusetts: "I need hardly say that all I can do to secure your triumphant election and a Republican victory will be done."

Hon. George C. Perkins, U. S. Senator, San Francisco, Cal.: "In behalf of the Republicans of California, I tender you my hearty congratulations and greet you as the foremost exponent of our party principles. We congratulate the people of our country that you will be our next President."

General Joseph R. Hawley. U. S. Senator, Hartford, Conn.: "We have a noble cause, a noble platform and a noble candidate. Sincerest congratulations and hearty support."

Hon. Francis E. Warren, U. S. Senator, Cheyenne, Wyoming: "Permit me to add my own to the sincere congratulations of Wyoming. It is the earnest purpose of the party in this State to add to its unanimous endorsement for nomination given you in State Convention some weeks since, its solid support at the polls next November."

Hon. Joseph B. Foraker, U. S. Senator-elect, Cincinnati, Ohio: "Heartiest congratulations upon your triumphant nomination."

Hon. J. C. Pritchard, U. S. Senator, Marshall, North Carolina: "Permit me to congratulate you on your nomination. I feel confident that you will receive the electoral vote of North Carolina."

Hon. Nelson W. Aldrich, United States Senator, Providence, Rhode Island: "I congratulate you that you are to have the post of honor and responsible leadership in the great contest for Protection and Sound Money. I believe the victory will be so emphatic that the policy we contend for will be accepted for a generation. I know how thoroughly your work will be a labor of love and how well it will always be done."

Hon. John M. Thurston, U. S. Senator, Omaha, Nebraska: "This is the year of the people."

Hon. John Sherman, U. S. Senator, Mansfield, Ohio: "My Dear Sir: I have not hurried in sending you my congratulations for your nomination as the next President of the United States, but they are not less hearty and sincere. I will gladly do all I can to secure your triumphant election. Give to Mrs. McKinley my best wishes, in which Mrs. Sherman joins."

Hon. John H. Mitchell, U. S. Senator from Oregon, Washington, D. C.: "Accept cordial congratulations."

Hon. Julius C. Burrows, U. S. Senator, Kalamazoo, Michigan: "Here's my hand and heart in sincerest congratulation! The nominees and platform will receive the triumphant endorsement of the American people."

Hon. Watson C. Squire, U. S. Senator, Seattle, Washington; "You have my earnest and hearty congratulations."

Hon. Jacob H. Gallinger, U. S. Senator, New Hampshire: "With pleasant memories of the Forty-Ninth and Fiftieth Congresses, and in anticipation of your triumphant election, I offer sincere congratulations."

Hon. Sereno E. Payne, M. C., Auburn, New York: "You have my most sincere congratulations, as you will have my heartiest support. New York is enthusiastic for the ticket, and I believe we will beat Pennsylvania majorities."

Hon. Warren B. Hooker, M. C., Fredonia, New York: "Hearty congratulations. This district will give you 16,000 plurality."

Hon. James H. Southard, M. C., Toledo, Ohio: "Accept heartiest congratulations. We also congratulate ourselves."

Hon. Winfield S. Kerr, M. C., Mansfield, Ohio: "Congratulations. The ovation when you were named was the greatest ever accorded an American citizen."

Hon. John Dalzell, M. C., Pittsburg, Pa.: "My congratulations and best wishes for your future success and happiness and that of our people."

Hon. Jonathan P. Dolliver, M. C., Fort Dodge: "Iowa is now to a man for you. My brother, Victor B. Dolliver, joins with me in greetings and congratulations to the Advance Agent of the Prosperity that is at hand."

Hon. Charles P. Taft, M. C., Cincinnati: "Accept my warmest congratulations on the results of the great Convention."

Hon. Matthew Griswold, M. C., Erie, Pa: "Congratulations. Honest Money and Protection will win the fight. Hurrah for the first victory!"

Hon. Walter Evans, M. C., Louisville, Ky.: "Accept my most cordial congratulations. I believe you will get the electoral vote of Kentucky."

General Charles A. Boutelle, M. C., Bangor, Maine: "Accept congratulations. If we could not have Reed, we are glad to raise the banner of Blaine's lifelong friend."

Hon. D. K. Watson, M. C., Columbus, Ohio: "Your nomination is the triumph of Protection; your election will be the triumph of Patriotism, and American homes will be the happier because of it. My congraulations on the great work of to-day."

Hon. Seth L. Milliken, M. C., Belfast, Maine: "Accept my sincere congratulations and give my regards to Hanna."

Hon. George W. Hulick, M. C., Batavia, Ohio: "I congratulate you and the party on your nomination, and the whole people of this country upon the promise of an Administration that will have for its guidance the patriotic principles so admirably enunciated in the St. Louis platform."

Hon. Joseph H. Walker, M. C., Worcester, Massachusetts: "Present to Mrs. McKinley and accept for yourself my most hearty congratulations."

Hon. Marriott Brosius, M. C., Lancaster, Pa.: "Lancaster County sends cordial congratulations."

Hon. Charles F. Joy, M. C., St. Louis: "Hearty congratulations. Command my services in any way to assist in compassing your triumphant election."

68

Hon. D. B. Henderson, M. C., Dubuque, Iowa: "Whipped but happy. Hearty and sincere congratulations."

Hon. **John A. Pickler**, M. C., Faulkton, S. D.: "Congratulations on your nomination and the vindication of the McKinley Bill, for which, under your leadership, I had the honor to vote. We will carry South Dakota for the Republican ticket, McKinley, Protection and Prosperity."

Hon. **Richmond Pearson**, M. C., Asheville, North Carolina: "McKinley, Protection and Prosperity nominated on first ballot. Accept congratulations."

Hon. **Lucien J. Fenton**, M. C., Winchester, Ohio.: "Hearty congratulation. Your triumph is the people's triumph."

Hon. **George Edmund Foss**, M. C., of Chicago: "The Convention was only a great ratification meeting."

Hon. **Nelson Dingley, Jr.**, M. C., Lewiston, Maine: "Congratulations. Maine Republicans were ardently for Reed until a majority made you the Republican standard bearer. They are now as earnestly for you."

Hon. **J. Frank Aldrich**, M. C., Chicago: "Congratulations and best wishes."

Hon. **John F. Lacey**, M. C., Oskaloosa, Iowa: "I congratulate you on your nomination and hope to be in the Fifty-Fifth Congress to support your administration."

Hon. **Edward S. Minor**, M. C., Sturgeon Bay, Wisconsin. from Washington: "Hearty congratulations. I leave for Wisconsin to enter at once on the campaign of 1896."

Hon. **Binger Herrman**, M. C., Roseburg, Oregon, from Elko, Nevada: "While crossing the continent to Oregon I have just learned of your nomination. Accept hearty congratulations."

Hon. **Joseph G. Cannon**, M. C., Danville, Illinois: "I heartily congratulate you upon your nomination."

Hon. **R. C. McCormick**, M. C., Jamaica, New York: "We believe your election is a foregone conclusion. Accept our warmest personal congratulations."

Mrs. Julia Dent Grant, widow of General Ulysses S. Grant, New York: "Accept congratulations for yourself and Mrs. McKinley."

Colonel and Mrs. Frederick D. Grant, New York: "We send to you, our future President, our heartfelt and joyful congratulations."

Mrs. U. S. Grant, Jr., San Diego, California: "Please accept my congratulations upon your nomination."

Webb C. Hayes, Cleveland, Ohio: "Hearty congratulations. We are perfectly delighted."

Mrs. Lucretia R. Garfield, widow of the late President James A. Garfield, Cleveland, Ohio, to Mrs. McKinley: "Our two families unite in congratulations to you and Major McKinley in the earnest hope that the next four years may bring to you the most of joy and the least of sorrow, and be made to the Nation years of triumphant prosperity."

Mrs. Harriet S. Blaine, widow of the late James G. Blaine, Augusta, Maine: "Hearty congratulations to yourself and Mrs. McKinley, with tender thoughts of the past."

Hon. **James G. Blaine, Jr.**, New York: "My hearty congratulations."

Hon. **John A. Logan, Jr.**, cabled from Copenhagen: "Hearty congratulations. All Americans abroad rejoice. Mother sends love to Mrs. McKinley."

Hon. **Russell B. Harrison**, Terre Haute, Indiana: "Please accept our

69

hearty congratulations on your nomination, which surely means success in November."

Mrs. Nathaniel P. Banks, widow of the first Republican Speaker of the National House of Representatives, Waltham, Mass.: "I rejoice in your nomination, and have confidence in your election."

Mrs. M. A. Hanna, Cleveland: "Happiest and warmest congratulations on your success."

Mrs. J. Ellen Foster, President Women's Republican Association of the United States, Geneseo, Illinois: "On behalf of two million American workingwomen I extend my heartiest congratulations."

Col. John Hay, one of President Lincoln's Private Secretaries, cabled from Lahaye: "Cordial greetings."

Judge Robert H. Douglas, son of the late Stephen A. Douglas, Greensboro, North Carolina: "Greetings and congratulations to the truest exponent of American interests."

Hon. Stephen A. Douglas, Chicago, Illinois: "McKinleyism, originated as a term of reproach, has become the only slogan of success."

Joseph Jefferson, Buzzard's Bay, Massachusetts: "I beg to offer my congratulations upon your nomination.

Richard Mansfield, Aurora, Illinois: "Accept my sincere congratulations."

Hon. Chauncey M. Depew, of New York: "I have attended many National conventions and never left one more perfectly satisfied with ticket and platform. I congratulate you on the honor, and the American people on the result."

Hon. M. A. Hanna, Judge Albert C. Thompson, and General Charles H. Grosvenor, Convention Hall, St. Louis: "Hearty congratulations. Never was there such enthusiasm before. No telling when Foraker can go on with his nominating speech. The Convention has been cheering you for thirty minutes."

Hon John Wanamaker, of Philadelphia, Pa., from Hoboken, N. J.: "Send this from the steamer, on which, at quarantine, I received good news. Hearty congratulations."

Hon. John W. Noble, ex-Secretary of the Interior, St. Louis: "Please accept my congratulations and my hope that you may be elected President. If we may redeem Missouri at the same time it will be additional cause for thanks and praise. The party has justice with it and is thrice armed."

Hon. Charles Foster, ex-Secretary of the Treasury, Fostoria, Ohio: "Your success is the most remarkable in many respects in our history. To all intents the nomination has perhaps more nearly the unanimity of the party behind it than any heretofore made."

Richard Hatton, New York: "A thousand congratulations from mother and myself."

Hon. Thomas L. James, ex-Postmaster General, New York: "Everybody shouts for McKinley and Hobart, Protection and Honest Money."

Hon. Thomas W. Ferry, ex-Senator and Acting Vice-President, Grand Haven, Michigan: "Accept my hearty congratulations upon the merited promptness of your Presidential nomination."

Hon. Samuel J. Randall, Chestnut Hill, Philadelphia: "Please accept my heartiest congratulations. Long live the Apostle of Patriotism, Protection and Prosperity!"

Hon. William L. Strong, Mayor, New York City: "New York will ratify your nomination in November by giving you the largest majority ever given a Presidential candidate."

Hon. Charles F. Warwick, Mayor, Philadelphia, Pa.: "Warmest congratulations."

General Powell Clayton, Eureka Springs, Arkansas: "The Republican masses have expressed themselves just as the masses of the people will at the polls."

Hon. Theodore Roosevelt, New York: "As a rule I do not like to prophecy, but I think it is safe to say New York will give you the largest majority by far that she has ever given a Presidential candidate."

Hon. John E. Russell, Boston, Massachusetts: "No man of all your admiring and·loving supporters more cordially and disinterestedly congratulates you and the country than I do. I am your sincere political opponent, but no less your cordial and sincere friend."

Hon. Frank Hiscock, Syracuse, New York: "I assure you of my very great personal satisfaction with your nomination. It was conducted in a most liberal spirit and with absolute fidelity to the principles of our party. We go into the canvass for your election unfettered by doubtful resolves and will gain a glorious triumph for our country. You have the right to be very proud of the love and respect of the American people for you."

Hon. H. Clay Evans, Planters Hotel, St. Louis: "Accept my congratulations. It was a great victory, and Tennessee was unanimously for you."

General Russell A. Alger, of Detroit, from the Convention Hall, St. Louis: "The entire Michigan delegation send greetings and congratulations to the next President."

Hon. John C. Spooner, ex-Senator, Madison, Wisconsin: "I congratulate you with all my heart upon the St. Louis consummation. Your nomination was really made long ago, and the Convention was merely a great National Committee appointed by the people to tender it to you. It will be a great pleasure to fight for such a ticket on such a platform."

Dr. John H. Vincent, Bishop of the Methodist Episcopal Church, congratulated Mrs. McKinley, saying: "You appreciate as no one else can, your husband's worth, nobility, power and tenderness."

Hon. John N. Dolph, of Portland, Oregon: "I congratulate you on your nomination and certain election."

General Granville M. Dodge, Des Moines, Iowa: "You have my hearty congratulations. As a true Iowan I will give you the heartiest support that lies in the power of an old comrade."

Hon. Blanche K. Bruce, ex-Senator from Mississippi, St. Louis: "For myself and people I heartily congratulate you."

Hon. William D. Washburn, of Minnesota, from the Convention Hall, St. Louis: "Heartiest congratulations on your nomination."

Charles Parsons, St. Louis: "Half my prophecy fulfilled, and remainder will be. Accept my warmest congratulations."

Hon. Tom Ochiltree, of Texas, cabled from London: "Sincere congratulations for yourself and our country."

Hon. John Patton, Jr., Grand Rapids, Michigan: "Heartiest congratulations to you and the country."

Hon. William P. Kellogg, of Louisiana, from St. Louis: "I may just as well send congratulations to you as President-elect."

Hon. John A. Sleicher, Albany: "All New York extends the glad hand to you."

Hon. Benjamin Butterworth, Washington, D. C.: "My wife and family

71

join me in congratulating you on the honor of having been named by the great Republican party for the highest office in the gift of a Nation of seventy millions of people."

Hon. L. E. McComas, U. S. Judge, Washington, D. C.: "I congratulate you on your unanimous nomination, so long foreseen, so well deserved. You will be President, a wise and safe one, well rounding out a great career. You will, I am sure, carry Maryland and other doubtful Southern States."

Col. W. W. Dudley, Washington, D. C.: "In common with all good Republicans I wish to send congratulations to you, because you deserve this great mark of confidence, and to the country, that your loyal, warm heart will control the destinies of the Republic for the next four years."

Hon. L. T. Michener, Washington, D. C.: "I congratulate you upon your nomination. I earnestly desire your election and will do whatever I can to accomplish that result."

Dr. Joseph Nimmo, Jr., Washington, D. C.: "I desire to congratulate you most cordially upon your nomination, and to express to you my most earnest hope and confident belief that if you live you will become President of the United States at high noon on the fourth of March next."

Thomas McDougall, Cincinnati: "You are candidate and platform, the great leader in the new era of peace and prosperity. Heartiest congratulations."

Hon. Nathan Goff, U. S. Judge, Washington, D. C.: "Accept congratulations. West Virginia will send greetings in November."

Hon. Milton G. Urner, ex-Congressman, Frederick, Maryland: "Please accept my cordial congratulations upon your splendid victory."

Hon. William E. Mason, Chicago: "It is done. Congratulations."

Judge P. S. Grosscup, Seattle, Washington: "Your second stage towards the White House is completed. November will finish the third. Congratulations."

Hon. Person C. Cheney, Manchester, N. H.: "Please accept my hearty congratulations."

Hon. John M. Langston, Petersburg, Virginia: "Congratulations and assurances of hearty support."

Hon. Morgan G. Bulkeley, Hartford, Connecticut: "Accept the hearty congratulations of the Connecticut delegation."

Hon. Albion Little, Portland, Maine: "You are clearly the choice of the people."

Hon. Benj. F. Jones, Pittsburg: "I beg to send my hearty congratulations on your nomination."

Hon. John W. Guffle, Fredricksburg, Virginia: "Republicans of this battle-scarred town recall with pleasure your service in the John S. Wise gubernatorial campaign and extend hearty congratulations."

Hon. Charles W. Fairbanks, Indianapolis, Indiana: "With all the warmth of my heart, I congratulate you upon the great honor that rests upon you, and which you so well deserve."

Hon. Morris M. Estee, San Francisco: "You will carry California."

Hon. James S. Clarkson, Des Moines, Iowa: "I congratulate you on your nomination and stand ready to do what I can to aid in making your success in November as triumphant as your success at St. Louis."

Hon. Charles R. Douglass, son of the distinguished colored orator, Frederick Douglass, Washington, D. C.: "As one of the host of American citizens who went to St. Louis for the purpose of securing your nomination to the highest office in the gift of the people, I desire to extend my congratulations and to promise my untiring support until the close of the polls on the day of election. My father, the late Frederick Douglass, had he lived until now, would be found in the forefront of your supporters. I only hope to be as true to the principles and candidates of the Republican party as he was."

Hon. L. B. Caswell, ex-Congressman, Fort Atkinson, Wisconsin: "The Convention did its work well. Accept most hearty congratulations."

Hon. John R. Buck, ex-Congressman, Hartford, Connecticut: "I congratulate you most heartily. You deserve it."

Emerson McMillen, New York: "The people breathe easier to-day than for many months past. With patriotism in high places, labor protected, and sound finance assured, prosperity will inevitably beam upon the country. Congratulations, in the full faith that the American voters will make you President."

Hon. James J. McKenna, United States Circuit Judge, San Francisco, California: "A crowning honor to a career of honor."

Hon. Wallace Bruce, United States Consul at Leith, Scotland: "The people are happy."

Dr. James H. Canfield, President of the Ohio State University, Columbus: "You may recall that I told you last fall that the result of the State election was a tribute to your personal hold upon the confidence of the people of this State. The result of the Convention at St. Louis simply carries this thought out to the people of the Nation. I have been a close observer of men and events for several years, and do not hesitate to say that you have won your own nomination by the strength of your character because the people believe in you."

Dr. T. P. Marsh, President Mount Union College, Alliance, Ohio: "Praise God from whom all blessings flow."

Hon. James T. Cutler, President of the Chamber of Commerce, Rochester, New York: "The party is to be congratulated. With such candidates and on such a platform we can not be beaten. I expect to renew my acquaintance with you during the campaign and hope to cast the vote of Monroe County for you in the electoral college, an honor and pleasure which in this case will be greatly enhanced by the personal esteem in which I hold you."

Howard P. Nash, Eminent Supreme Recorder, Northport, New York: "The entire Sigma Alpha Epsilon fraternity send congratulations to the next President of the United States."

H. D. Julliard, New York City: "The business interests and industrial welfare of the whole country are to be congratulated on your nomination and assured election. Prosperity will speedily return to us on the wings of Protection and Sound Finance."

Hon. John G. Sawyer, Albion, N. Y.: "The people will confirm the action of the Convention by an unprecedented majority."

Hon. Daniel H. Hastings, Governor, and Hon. H. C. McCormick, Attorney General, of Pennsylvania: "Pennsylvania rejoices at your nomination, and we personally extend you our heartiest congratulations."

Hon. A. S. Bushnell, Governor of Ohio, St. Louis: "I congratulate you, Ohio, and the whole people of the United States on your nomination for the Presidency."

Hon. John W. Griggs, Governor, Paterson, New Jersey: "We congratulate you. Ohio and New Jersey will be joined in the most prosperous Administration our country has ever had."

Hon. Lloyd Lowndes, Governor, Annapolis, Maryland: ". congratulate you and tender best wishes for your success."

Hon. E. N. Morrill, Governor of Kansas, Topeka: "I congratulate you with all my heart on the magnificent endorsement you have received from the people of our country. I feel sure that it will be ratified by an immense majority at the polls, and that you will give us one of the ablest and purest Administrations that the country has ever known. We shall work from now on until the election night, to give you a good majority in this State. May God give you strength to sustain you in the discharge of the arduous duties which will devolve upon you."

Hon. Urban A. Woodbury, Governor of Vermont, Burlington: "The country is to be congratulated. I predict your triumphant election and the return of prosperity. Vermont will set the pace in September."

Hon. Charles W. Lippett, Governor of Rhode Island, from St. Louis: "Congratulations to Mrs. McKinley and yourself upon the grand results of the day."

Hon. Daniel L. Russell, Republican candidate for Governor, Willmington: "North Carolina will ratify your nomination with eleven electoral votes in the right column."

Hon. L. K. Fuller, ex-Governor of Vermont, Brattleboro: "My heartiest congratulations and best wishes. Vermont is as true as the stars of heaven in this great work. Victory is within our reach. God bless and keep you."

Hon. D. Russell Brown, ex-Governor of Rhode Island, St. Louis: "Accept heartiest congratulations and earnest wishes for your election."

Hon. Arthur Thomas, ex-Governor, Salt Lake City, Utah: "Accept my hearty, sincere and earnest congratulations."

Hon. Charles T. Sexton, Lieutenant Governor, Clyde, New York: "Hearty congratulations to our next President."

Hon. William II. Haile, Lieutenant Governor of Massachusetts, Springfield: "You will be triumphantly elected."

Hon. John Palmer, Secretary of State, Albany: "Hearty congratulations. McKinley and Protection touch the hearts of the people of New York."

Hon. Richard Dallam, Secretary of State, Annapolis, Md.: "Ticket and platform invincible. You are sure of Maryland's electoral vote."

Hon. Joseph Flory, State Railroad Comissioner, St. Louis: "Missouri was solid for you to-day and will be in November."

Hon. M. J. Dowling, Secretary of the National Republican League of the United States: "Pursuant to a resolution unanimously adopted at the meeting of our Executive Committee in the city of St. Louis, I have the honor of tendering you the best wishes of the National Republican League, representing a volunteer army of working Republicans numbering more than two million members, many of whom will cast their first vote for McKinley and Hobart."

Hotel Brotherhood, Philadelphia, Pa.: "The colored people rejoice at your nomination."

Charles H. Holmes, President, Boston, Mass.: "Chelsea organized a McKinley and Hobart Club to-night. Motto: 'Clear the track for Major Mack, for the good old times are coming back.'"

E. C. DeWitt, President, and seven hundred members, Marquette Club, Chicago: "We pledge you our most active and earnest support in the campaign upon which we are entering, to the end that the People's Choice may prevail, and the principles of the Grand Old Party, as set forth in the platform on which you stand, may be established."

Capt. John K. Gowdy, Chairman Republican State Executive Committee, Rushville, Indiana: "Accept my hearty congratulations. The people have spoken and they will speak again in November."

Hon. A. M. Higgins, President of the Indiana Republican League: "Indiana thirty for McKinley at St. Louis. She will add three ciphers in November."

Hon. Scott Swetland, Chairman Republican State Central Committee, Vancouver, Washington: "In the name of the Republicans of the State of Washington, I wish to heartily congratulate you."

Hon. William B. Thorpe, Secretary California McKinley League, Sacramento: "California will give you a rousing majority."

James A. Doyle, William Armstrong and Henry Roberts, Anaconda, Colorado: "Accept our hearty congratulations from the greatest gold camp on earth."

John S. Lentz, President Massachusetts Car Builders, and S. C. Blackell, President Massachusetts Mechanics, in session at Saratoga: "Hearty congratulations, fifteen hundred strong, to our next President."

C. A. Perkins, Chairman National Committee American College League: "We will do everything in our power to roll up a big majority for the Advocate of Protection."

Hon. Samuel J. Roberts, Chairman Republican State Executive Committee, Lexington, Kentucky, from Convention Hall, St. Louis: "We are shouting ourselves hoarse. The hopes of many years have resulted in great joy."

Hon. Frank M. Laughlin, Chairman Republican State Central Committee, San Francisco: "The Republicans of California congratulate you and promise their unqualified support at the polls of our united party pledged to to Protection and Prosperity."

William J. Muston, President, Pittsburg, Pa.: "The Americus Republican Club extends to its honored fellow member sincerest congratulations, and pledges its heartiest support, and a repetition of its triumphs of 1888 in great parades."

L. F. Cain, President, Elwood Indiana: "The Elwood City Republican League Club and 4,000 factory laborers send greetings to the next President of the United States."

J. K. Merrifield, Union Depot, Kansas City, Missouri: "The laboring men nominated you. Now they will elect you."

W. A. Rodenberg, and J. D. Gerlach, St. Louis: "Hearty congratulations. The Twenty-First Illinois Congressional District will give you 5,000 majority."

J. T. McNeely, Cripple Creek, Colorado: "The Republican Party still lives and thousands of Colorado Republicans are panting for the chance to vote for you."

Hon. Eben S. Draper, Chairman, for the Massachusetts delegation, and one hundred others, Buffalo, New York: "The Massachusetts delegation, returning from the most important Republican National Convention since the war, congratulate you upon the unanimity and enthusiasm of your nomination, and congratulate the country upon having at this crisis a leader who in private life, public experience and administrative ability commands universal confidence. We take this occasion to pledge our unswerving loyalty and hearty devotion until the votes of all sections of the country proclaim you President of the United States."

Harvey H. Lindley, Chairman, and Daniel T. Cole, Vice Chairman, California delegation, St. Louis: "At a meeting of the California delegation, this morning, we were authorized to extend our united and cordial congratulations on your nomination, and to assure you of California's electoral vote."

Messrs. Charles W. Parrish, Chairman, Charles B. Hilton, Robert A. Booth, Charles S. Moore, John W. Heldmon, John F. Calbreath, Charles H. Dodd, Wallace McCamant, Convention Hall, St. Louis: "The Oregon delegation congratulates the Nation on your nomination. We pledge every possible effort for your election."

Col. I. N. Walker, National Commander Grand Army of the Republic, Indianapolis, Indiana: "Earnest congratulations. Our patriotic people always do the right thing."

Captain George C. James, National Commander of the Union Veteran Legion, of the United States, Cincinnati, Ohio: "Sincere congratulations and best wishes for the happiness of both Mrs. McKinley and yourself."

Capt. W. H. Chamberlain, Commander of the Loyal Legion of Ohio, Cincinnati: "Dear Sir and Companion—While politics by the organic law has no place in this Order, there is no prohibition against the expression of natural pride when the people of the United States thrice make requisition upon the Ohio Commandery for a Chief Magistrate of the Republic."

Major J. L. Dobbin, President Union Veterans Legion, Minneapolis, Minnesota: "Your comrades of the Union Veterans Legion of this city have by resolution directed me to tender you their hearty congratulations, pledge their earnest support, and say that the North Star State will give you 50,000 majority next November."

Edward Everett Henry, Chicago: "Our beloved commander, General Rutherford B. Hayes, one day said to me, 'Mark it, some day Major McKinley will be President.' In the name of our famous old regiment I give you twenty-three cheers. Your election is assured."

D. V. Wherry, Shelby, Ohio, whose message is one of forty or fifty from Major McKinley's old comrades of the Twenty-Third Ohio, in all parts of the country: "Another battle fought, another victory won, with the old Twenty-Third well to the front. Congratulations."

Hon. William Lawrence, President Wool Growers National Association, Bellefontaine, Ohio: "Congratulations. A million wool growers have occasion to rejoice. Better pay our gold to our wool growers than to send it to foreigners."

William G. Markham, Secretary of the National Wool Growers Association, Rochester, New York: "I congratulate you, as well as the wool growers and our country, at the result in St. Louis."

Charles Emory Smith, Philadelphia, Pa.: "You have my profound and heartfelt congratulations at your majestic triumph in a great cause of which you are the chosen leader."

H. H. Kohlsaat, Chicago: "Congratulations for yourself and wife."

Joseph B. McCullagh, Editor of the Globe Democrat, St. Louis: "Accept my heartiest congratulations."

M. H. DeYoung, San Francisco, Cal.: "Hearty congratulations. Hope soon to greet you with the title of President."

R. C. Alexander, Editor of the Mail and Express, New York: "On the eve of a notable and an honorable victory I send greetings and congratulations. I think I speak with reverence in saying we have fought a good fight, and, better still, have kept the faith."

Edward Rosewater, Proprietor of The Bee, Omaha: "Accept sincere congratulations. We propose to hold Nebraska in line and feel confident she will stand by Protection and Sound Money against all combinations."

George Alfred Townsend, the noted newspaper correspondent "GATH," from Gapland, Maryland: "The army correspondents laid their corner-stone on South Mountain, Maryland, while you were being nominated. Come back here where you served hot coffee to your regiment and dedicate our memorial as President-elect."

Hon. R. G. Horr, The Tribune, New York: "I desire to express my great satisfaction with the entire work of the St. Louis Convention. Accept my hearty congratulations."

D. C. O'Malley, Proprietor Daily Item, New Orleans: "The vote of Louisiana next November will indicate that when it comes to McKinley and Protection there is no North and no South, but a common cause and country. Success to the Republican ticket."

John Addison Porter, Editor of Evening Post, Hartford, Connecticut: "You will receive the electoral vote of the Nutmeg State by the largest majority ever cast for a Presidential candidate."

Melville D. Landon, "Eli Perkins," New York: "Now the mills will start, workmen work, deficit cease, debt decrease, importations diminish, gold stay at home, and prosperity come back again. Arise and sing!"

James Arkell, "Judge," New York City: "Not you alone, but the whole country is to be congratulated on your nomination."

W. W. Baker, Editor, Portland, Oregon: "The Farmer and Stockman begs to congratulate you and the country."

W. W. Burch, Editor American Sheep Breeder and Wool Grower, Chicago: "We voice congratulations and godspeed from one million American wool growers."

POLITICAL CLUBS AND PATRIOTIC ASSOCIATIONS.

Thirty-Fifth Ward Republican Club, Cleveland, Ohio.
The Lenox Republican Club, New York City.
Union League Club, San Francisco, California.
Frederick Douglass Republican Association, Pittsburg, Pa.
Lincoln Club, Brooklyn, N. Y.
Gattling Gun Battery, Cleveland, Ohio.
McKinley Club, Detroit, Michigan.
National Potters' Association, Trenton, New Jersey.
Sixth Ward Republican Club, Baltimore, Maryland.
German-American Lincoln Club, Baltimore, Md.
McKinley Club, Davenport, Iowa.
Blaine Club, Twenty-Fifth Assembly District, New York City.
Young Men's Republican Association, Jersey City, N. J.
Republican Club, Buffalo, New York.
Citizens' McKinley League, Thirty-Seventh Ward, Philadelphia, Pa.
McKinley and Hobart Campaign Club, Baltimore, Md.
The Ohio Club, Cleveland, Ohio.
Republican Club, Twenty-Second Assembly District, New York City.
McKinley League, New York City.
Republican Club, Jacksonville, Florida.
Italian Benevolent Society Cincinnati, Ohio.
McKinley League, Thirty-Fifth Assembly District, New York City.
Republican Club, New Brighton, Pa.

McKinley Club, Homestead, Pa.
Marion Club, Indianapolis, Pa.
McKinley Club, Frankfort, Kentucky.
McKinley League, Mt. Vernon, Ohio.
McKinley Club, Hartford, Connecticut.
Union Veterans League, Minneapolis, Minn.
Republican Club, Covington, Kentucky.
Republican State Editorial Association, Jackson, Michigan.
Republican National League, Chicago.
German-American Republicans of the Northwest, St. Paul.
Car Builders' Convention, Saratoga, New York.
McKinley Ratification Meeting, Donaldsonville, La.
Company G, 10th O. N. G., Wauseon, Ohio.
Union League Club, San Franciso, California.
McKinley League, Sixteenth Assembly District, Brooklyn, N. Y.
Tippecanoe Club, Cleveland, Ohio.
New Amsterdam Republican Club, New York.
Champion Lodge, Knights of Pythias, Columbus, Ohio.
Garfield Club, Hamilton, Ohio.
McKinley League. New York.
American College Republican League, New York.
McKinley League, Onondaga County, New York.
Republican State Committee. Birmingham, Alabama.
Business Men's Republican Club, Zanesville. Ohio.
A. C. Harmer Club. Fifth Congressional District, Pennsylvania.
Pittsburg Coal Exchange, Pittsburg, Pa.
Sand Plains Republican Club, Parkersburg, West Virginia.
McKinley and Hobart Club, Ottumwa, Iowa.
Fifteenth Ward Republican Club, Milwaukee, Wisconsin.
McKinley Club, Spokane, Washington.
R. C. McKinney Club, Hamilton, Ohio.
Republican Executive Committee of Greene County, Xenia, Ohio.
McKinley Guards, Urbana, Ohio.
Republicans Eighth Congressional District, Williamsburg, Ky.
McKinley League, Richmond County, New York.
McKinley League, Philadelphia Pa.
McKinley Club, Walla Walla. Washington.
McKinley League, Albany County, New York.
Sixth Ward Central Republican Club, Baltimore, Md.
Republican Committee, Fulton County, Johnstown, N. Y.
Seventh Ward Republican League, Kansas City, Mo.
Central McKinley Club. Knoxville, Tenn.
McKinley Ratification Meeting. North Tonawanda, N. Y.
McKinley Club, Ottawa, Illinois.
McKinley and Hobart Club, Wahoo, Nebraska.
McKinley and Hobart Club, Dewitt, Nebraska.
McKinley Club, Plattsmouth, Nebraska.
Unconditional Republican Club, Albany, N. Y.
Thirty-Fifth Ward McKinley Club, Cleveland, Ohio.
Home Market Club, Boston, Massachusetts.
Young Men's Republican Club, Philadelphia, Pa.
Lincoln Club, Twenty-Sixth Ward, Brooklyn, N. Y.

McKinley Ratification Meeting, Oneida, N. Y.
McKinley Club, Garrettsville, Ohio.
Ohio Club, Norfolk, Nebraska.
Standard Republican Club, Fifth Ward, Louisville, Ky.
Eighth Ward Hebrew Political Club, Pittsburg, Pa.
McKinley Club, Wellsville, Ohio.
Hamilton Club, Chicago, Ill.
McKinley Club, Owensboro, Ky.
United Republican Association, Philadelphia, Pa.
Cassius M. Barnes McKinley Club, Guthrie, Oklahoma.
Francis F. Williams Eighteenth Ward Republican Battery, Brooklyn, N. Y.
Charlestown Republican Club, Bunker Hill, Boston, Mass.
Twentieth Assembly District Republicans, Brooklyn, N. Y.
Republican Committee Queen's County, Minnesota, N. Y.
McKinley Club, Indianapolis, Ind.
Detroit McKinley Club, Detroit, Mich.
Albany Republican League, Albany, Mich.
McKinley Club, Arcanum, Ohio.
McKinley Club, Nero Springs, Iowa.
Lafayette Battery, Jersey City, N. J.
Buffalo Republican League, Buffalo, N. Y
Montauk Club, Brooklyn, N. Y.
Quigg Club, New York, N. Y.
Continental League, San Francisco, California.
Union League Club, Philadelphia, Pa.
Stalwart Republican Club, Nashville, Tenn.
McKinley Republican Club, Pullman, Ill.
Commercial Travelers' Republican Club, Indianapolis, Ind.
Robert J. Wright Republican Club, New York.
Republican Central Committee, Atoka, Indian Territory.
People of Canton, Pennsylvania.
McKinley Club, Fort Dodge, Iowa.
McKinley Club, Ashtabula, Ohio.
McKinley Club, Lyons, New York.
Madison County McKinley Club, London, Ohio.
Young Men's Republican Club, Jamestown, N. Y.
McKinley Club, Lockport, New York.
West Side Republican Club, New York.
Young Republicans' Thurston Club, Omaha, Nebraska.
McKinley Club, Newark, New Jersey.
McKinley Club, Hartford, Connecticut.
Citizens' McKinley League, Thirty-Seventh Ward, Philadelphia, Pa.
Republican Executive Committee, Fulton County, Atlanta, Georgia.
Cleveland Grays, Cleveland, Ohio.
Forsyth Republican Club, Winston, North Carolina.
McKinley Republican League, Muscotah, Kansas.
McKinley Republican League, Lockport, New York.
Marketmen's Republican Club, Boston, Massachusetts.
Ross County Republican Executive Committee, Chillicothe, Ohio.
McKinley Club, Westfield, New York.   ------
Chemung County Republican Committee, Elmira, New York.
National Republican Club, Washington, D. C.

Young Men's Republican Club, Hebron, Nebraska
McKinley Club, Green Falls, New York.
Young Men's Republican Club, Zanesville, Ohio.
Columbia Club, Indianapolis, Ind.
Fellowship Club, Chicago, illinois.
Maine Woolen Manufacturers' Club, Sanford, Maine.
Young Men's Republican Club, Lebanon, Indiana.
McKinley Club, Waco, Texas.
Lincoln Club, Chicago, Illinois.
Marquette Club, Chicago, Illinois.
McKinley and Hobart Club, Chelsea, Mass.
Black Belt McKinley Club, Selma, Alabama.
McKinley Club, Covington, Indiana.
McKinley and Hobart Club, Canton, New York.
McKinley League, Fordham, New York.
Republican Central Committee, of Clarke County, Springfield, Ohio.
Frederick Douglass Republican Association, Pittsburg, Pa.
Blaine Club, Twenty-Fifth Assembly District, New York City.
R. B. Hayes Club, Twenty-Third O. V. I., Cleveland, Ohio.
McKinley Club, Springer, New Mexico.
Marion Club, Indianapolis, Indiana.
Republican Club, Twenty-Second Assembly District, New York City.
German-American Lincoln Club, Baltimore, Md.
Cambro-American Republican Club, Columbus, Ohio.
Michigan Club, Detroit, Mich.
Young Men's Republican Tariff Club, Pittsburg, Pa.
Canby Post, No. 27, G. A. R., Ilwaco, Washington.
Thomas B. Reed Club, Biddeford, Maine.
Frances Harper League, Pittsburg, Pa.
McKinley League, Mt. Vernon, New York.
McKinley Club, Frankfort, Kentucky.
Republican League, Jacksonville, Florida.
West End McKinley Republican Club, Washington, D. C.
McKinley League, Syracuse, New York.
McKinley Club, Evansville, Indiana.
Capital City McKinley Club, Albany, New York.
McKinley Club, Peru, Indiana.
Newark Republican Club, Newark, Ohio.
Young Men's Republican Association, Jersey City, N. J.
Republican Club, Modelia, Minnesota
McKinley Club, Springfield, Illinois.
Tacoma Republican Club, Tacoma, Washington.
Cuba Post, Grand Army of the Republic, Cuba, N. Y.
Garfield Club, Urbana, Ohio.
French-American Republican Club, Marlboro, Mass.
The Americus Republican Club, Pittsburg, Pa.
Hardin County Republican Committee, Kenton, Ohio.
Elwood Republican League Club, Elwood, Ind.
Union Republican Club, Washington, D. C.
McKinley Ratification Meeting, New Orleans.